MAGGIE
A GIRL OF

THE FIRST NOVEL LIBRARY

Maggie

A GIRL OF THE STREETS

STEPHEN CRANE

EDITED BY HERBERT VAN THAL

WITH AN

INTRODUCTION

BY

WILLIAM SANSOM

CASSELL   LONDON

CASSELL & COMPANY LTD
35 Red Lion Square, London WC1
Melbourne, Sydney, Toronto
Johannesburg, Cape Town, Auckland

Introductory material © Cassell & Co. Ltd, 1966
First published in 1892
First published in this edition, 1966

*Set in Monotype Garamond type and
printed in Great Britain by Cox & Wyman Ltd,
London, Reading and Fakenham*
F. 666

THE FIRST NOVEL LIBRARY

WHAT is a novel? This pertinent question has been answered by a considerable number of critics, writers and novelists. One of our most admirable and eminent critics, Walter Allen points out in his excellent survey *The English Novel* 'Like any other artist the novelist is a maker. He is making an imitation of the life of man on earth.'

The novelist creates characters according to his view of life, and he creates a story around these characters, or a study—whether it is to inculcate right conduct, to reform manners, expose evils, social or otherwise—for an almost endless variety of purposes. He may set out merely to entertain, a thing many an admirable novelist has successfully done, winning multitudes of admirers. The novelist is also expected by his readers to be 'true to life', or he can, like Defoe, our first great novelist, benevolently hoodwink his public by declaring his narrative to be true. We often use the old cliché 'truth is strange than fiction', but then we can assert with equal truth that fiction is often stranger than truth, and is none the worse for that. J. E. Baker has said,[1] 'The regular prose method is to put together a larger, more complex, more eccentric, or more subtle being out of the raw materials supplied by life. We recognize the creator's truth at every step, but the cumulative result exceeds anything within our ken.' The novelist may pursue his art as a most meticulous craftsman, and become one of the greatest influences on the modern novel, as did Henry James, or become an innovator of style and language as did James Joyce. The popularity of Dickens lay in his ability to create characters larger than life. On the other hand, as Somerset Maugham

[1] *History of the English Novel,* Vol. i. p. 20.

has said, 'A writer seldom writes as he would like to; he writes as he can; he is often aware of his defects; but he can rid himself of them as little as he can change the colour of his eyes.' The present series encompasses every conceivable variety of the form, from the founder of the English novel to the day before yesterday. There is, however, a unique difference in this series in that every author is represented by his first work. Was that work indicative of what was to come? Could one forecast from his first novel his development or decline? The Introductions to the volumes, written by experts, seek to answer these questions by giving the reader a survey of each chosen novelist by determining how his or her art evolved; what kind of a 'tree' resulted from those 'roots'? Those who became famous later in their careers and those whose total achievement brought them less fame are included in this Library of First Novels.

HERBERT VAN THAL

INTRODUCTION

by WILLIAM SANSOM

A GIRL OF THE STREETS! The story of a falling woman
crosses our sky once again.

Maggie begins as a very young girl of the streets, she
has her springtime of purity 'blossoming in a mud puddle'.
She encounters temptation, tries to put the wrong people
right in the face of fearful odds, fails, and ends as a girl
no longer of but on the streets.

For once this familiar Victorian journey is told not in
pious terms but with the realist pen of a modern journalist.
The writer knew from the first that a story is not only
what happens and why, but more importantly *how* it
happens. It is the observance of that 'how' which brings
a tale like *Maggie* to life. Rum Alley is a well-worn subject:
it takes a writer of Crane's stature to represent its immedi-
acy, to show us not the cliché of a drunken father but
exactly what a room looks like when he has passed
through it.

Stephen Crane has been forgotten many times. He began by being forgotten. As a young journalist he had to
publish *Maggie* at his own expense and saw it plunge
instantly into long oblivion. But a year or two later he
sold for publication a second novel, *The Red Badge of
Courage*, which was eventually to ring the bell. An un-
usually honest examination of the mixture of fear and
courage in a soldier's experience of war, and of war's
hour-to-hour waste and boredom, the book was not at
first well received in an America which had suffered the
war well within living memory; but in 1896 it was

exceptionally well received in an England which had not suffered such a war. Interest in America was revived. Success! Yet Crane wrote no further novel. In the next few years before his death he worked as a roving war correspondent; and at least from these experiences came the many famous short stories.

A prose writer of small output tends to be forgotten fairly quickly. He has neither the jewelled compaction of a poet, nor the reiterative production of the usual novelist who keeps his name in front of the public and his head above water in much the same manner as reminder-advertising works: name more important than story. Crane provided no such rhythmic reminder-fodder and he got forgotten.

Then the Kaiser's War came. And *The Red Badge of Courage* was posthumously revived into a best-seller. It showed the pity of the common soldier's lot, it also showed the reality of words like courage and loyalty, words over-used at the tea-table and recruiting station. It was even a book for soldiers, a textbook of how to get over your first battle and fight happily ever afterwards.

Came the peace, and Crane was forgotten again. It took Hitler to revive him, together with a motion picture industry heartened by the success of another Civil War story, *Gone with the Wind*. Thus we have Crane's *Prelude in C sharp minor*, overawing his other work, repeatedly rescuing him from oblivion. Let us now resuscitate the true prelude, his first book, and try this time not to forget.

We are in a tough Irish quarter of New York in the ebullient eighties, among families ghettoed by poverty into packed tenements, whose only relief from long hours of hard labour is a combination of fist and bottle. Both Maggie's father and mother are drunks, regularly wreck a home made up of a few pitiful sticks, beat their children and kill the baby by neglect. It is a mud puddle all right.

Yet . . . for the teenage Maggie only a few unattainable cents separate this perpetual drab prison from a sort of heaven made of the pink seat in a ninth-rate music-hall, and the beautiful glamour of a pair of cheap patent leather shoes.

Only a few cents . . . and where do they come from? They come to her—almost as magically as Cinderella's coach—from the pocket of a flash young bhoyo with an oiled bang, whose 'patent leather shoes looked like weapons'. A friend of her brother's, no more than a barman, at puddle level he is Prince Charming in person— and Maggie falls not only for him but for the chance of pleasanter atmospheres. No nonsense about preferring love at all costs—like any girl today she goes for the boy but also the motor-scooter. Or on a darker note, a pretty dress and release from a dull job become a dream attained —the prime reason for all prostitution.

So Maggie is tempted: but does not easily fall. Her innocence makes even the brazen bhoyo quite tender—he takes her to museums. Only occasionally does he burst out, in the unspoken words of the foot-weary in search of culture, 'Aw! Look at all dese little jugs! Hundred jugs in a row! . . . What d'blazes use is dem?' In fact, he is a reasonable and round character too. Crane paints them both objectively and without emotion. He is passionate only about the circumstances of poverty and human frailty which drive forward the situation. When a dreadful outburst from Maggie's drunken mother finally forces her into the young man's protection and bed, this critical moment in a girl's life is economized into two words: 'Maggie went.'

Thereafter a few rosier weeks for sad Maggie—'She did not feel like a bad woman. To her knowledge she had never seen any better.' But soon her softness and devotion to Pete lets her down. Pete meets and prefers a more sophisticated woman. Maggie is out, returns home, is again thrown out by her mother, and life in the streets begins in earnest.

This life is not dwelt upon. It begins its pathetic realism with the girl alone on the street, abandoned by everyone, saying to herself simply the one word, 'Who?' It is as practical a question as might be 'What now?' when anyone has missed the last train and has to think of a hotel room. No alternative. And after this, silent secret weeks elapse until, with the abruptness of a shock film cut, Maggie reappears in the full paint and colour of a sacrificial victim in the dreadful and beautiful Chapter 17, an extraordinarily fine essay of dramatic restraint and the epitome of Crane's carefully oblique approach.

For this whole book has the subtle attitude of a writer who is passionately in earnest about his story, who will drum and drum on certain consonant atmospheres, but who gracefully declines to dramatize the highest moments; who leaves them to the finest of all statements, silence and implication. What is left out is as important as what is put in. Salt and pepper the reader's mind, entice it with rare herbs—and let him do the rest. It is the technique of much great painting.

It is also, curiously, for us today, a reaffirmation of the value of the dotted line which used to imply the sexual act. Sex and eating are ordinary animal functions, their description is dull. Who wants a meal described unless there is an emotional echo in the toast beneath the ptarmigan? Who wants to know how A's legs wrap themselves around B's—unless something making for much greater pregnancy is said at the same time? Similarly the pure violence of a large dramatic moment is heightened by restriction: the preparatory ponderings of Hamlet are much more important than the coda of sword thrusts.

Crane is from the first most concerned with setting his thematic background—Life the Villain—and does not introduce his adult heroine until page 19 and leaves her on page 74 with a good eight pages to run on, enough to make a movie-man turn in his own spool. The whole book is conceived as a frame of poverty and boozy delinquence within whose knuckled ivory and red-wine plush the moving oleograph of Maggie's life bursts into colour and gradually fades. It is an oblique technique, and succeeds beautifully in its mixture of passionate over-statement, emotional discipline.

Even in the middle of this story within a set-piece a further story comes to interrupt Maggie's Odyssey. It is the description in detail of a fight between her brother and her fancyman: drama within drama, and here intro-duced both to divert from Maggie herself and to empha-size again the harshness of life, and in Crane's paradoxical fashion even to glorify it as he loathes it, just as he glorifies the Irish–Catholic religiosity of the hag-mother whose scruples of decent behaviour can throw Mag into the street while she herself is indecently drunk but within the acceptable bounds of the roaring bottle. The glory is that this is the way people behave, they have their reasons, life is like this. In *The Red Badge of Courage*, Crane similarly accepts, and implicitly praises, both expedient cowardice and run-of-the-mill bravery. He echoes this in *The Veteran*, a short story of a man who remembers his fear in war and the next moment sacrifices his life in a fire. And Maggie's innocence in a drunken home is echoed in *The Little Dog*, a further essay on the thought-less, brutish behaviour of people whom Crane cannot bring to himself to rebuke for not knowing better; for how can they? Life is like that, and life is weighted against them.

The prose itself reveals a wish to be direct at most costs. The description of a music-hall begins: 'An orchestra of yellow silk women and bald-headed men,' etc. Not women *in* yellow silk. And in the middle of a smoking, packed description of the music-hall audience, he refers suddenly to 'very infrequent tipsy men'. A less honest writer would never have bothered with that 'infrequent' which lowers the raciness but solidifies the truth. Against such exactness, Crane excusably falls into some of the traps of the ponderous journalese of the period, prose of the Latin-bred preacher. 'She divulged the fact that she was attired in some half-dozen skirts.' There is a lot of this, but one feels all the time that he is fighting against it, and the battle is always won with such effectively simple definitions as that of Maggie's corner-boy brother: 'Jimmie's occupation for a long time was to stand at street corners and watch the world go by, dreaming blood-red dreams at the passing of pretty women. He menaced mankind at the intersections of streets.'

That last sentence has a masterly French ring, an echo of Baudelaire. And of the same young brother Jimmie, he rounds off the hardness of a brutalized mind with sudden soft sympathy, 'Nevertheless, he had, on a certain star-lit evening, said wonderingly and quite reverently, "Deh moon looks like hell, don't it?"'

There are other echoes of the masters. At a climactic moment on the tattered tenement landing, when, surrounded by jeering neighbours, Maggie's figure stands lonely and lost as her raging mother shouts and shuts her out, 'A baby, overcome with curiosity concerning this object at which all were looking, sidled forward and touched her dress, cautiously, as if investigating a red-hot stove.' Dostoievsky?

And then this economical writer of short books and short sentences takes a risk which few writers would dare. To keep to the truth of Bowery dialogue, he uses a dangerous transliteration, and drums it home, risking at the same time all the unacceptability of printed dialect and the repetitious boredom of a crude character's mind. From the boasting teeth of Maggie's bhoyo with

xii

his oiled lock of hair: 'Hully gee!' says he, 'dose mugs can't feaze me. Dey knows I kin wipe up d'street wid any tree of dem.' And he says it again and again and again. Astoundingly, it works. It is absolutely sincere. It is never commented upon. It is. And one is reminded how Edgar Allan Poe, in another way, used this shameless repetition to drum and drum home what was foremost in his mind. Like drumming itself, it works best when overworked.

For us reading *Maggie* today there are also a few period perks. Early references to the drinking of 'cocktails' in bars of the 'eighties (but we remember that Toulouse-Lautrec painted 'cocktail' drinking and an Irish American bar in the Paris of his time); and forgotten niceties such as electric lights 'whirring softly'; and the buttonholing of the chrysanthemum by dandies in evening dress. It all makes for a general suspension of disbelief. What is not so believable is, for instance, the continual breaking up of a very poor family's furniture. How is it replaced? Crane does not say. I do not think he even knew. Just as he gives Maggie's Pete, a working bar-tender, far too much free time off. Crane wrote *The Red Badge of Courage* from hearsay, from the tales of living veterans. He comes through from the outside with an absolutely believable piece of realism. But heaven knows how many real errors there may not be in such a book. In the case of Maggie we are much nearer the observed truth. There seem to be only the above two trifling inconsistencies, both excusable as dramatic licence.

But above all else, the book succeeds on a human note. It is a great sympathetic portrait of a poor, hopeful, finally hopeless young woman, painted without one maudlin note.

Maggie, A Girl of the Streets, published in London as *A Child of the Streets*, was published in America in 1839. The author was then a part-time journalist, aged twenty-two, youngest of fourteen sons of a Methodist moralist preacher and writer. In 1895 the up and down journey of *The Red Badge of Courage* began. Thereafter Crane became a reporter for one of the earliest newspaper syndicates, got shipwrecked off Cuba and married in Greece. With his wife, née Cora Taylor, he came to London and the circle of H. G. Wells and Joseph Conrad. From Oxted in Surrey he went off to cover the Spanish–American War in Cuba, and returned in 1899 to Brede Place near Rye. He died of consumption in 1900 at Badenweiler in the Black Forest, at the age of only twenty-eight.

CHAPTER 1

A VERY little boy stood upon a heap of gravel for the honour of Rum Alley. He was throwing stones at howling urchins from Devil's Row, who were circling madly about the heap and pelting him.

His infantile countenance was livid with the fury of battle. His small body was writhing in the delivery of oaths.

'Run, Jimmie, run! Dey'll git yehs!' screamed a retreating Rum Alley child.

'Naw,' responded Jimmie with a valiant roar, 'dese mugs can't make me run.'

Howls of renewed wrath went up from Devil's Row throats. Tattered gamins on the right made a furious assault on the gravel heap. On their small convulsed faces shone the grins of true assassins. As they charged, they threw stones and cursed in shrill chorus.

The little champion of Rum Alley stumbled precipitately down the other side. His coat had been torn to shreds in a scuffle and his hat was gone. He had bruises on twenty parts of his body, and blood was dripping from a cut in his head. His wan features looked like those of a tiny insane demon.

On the ground, children from Devil's Row closed in on their antagonist. He crooked his left arm defensively about his head and fought with madness. The little boys ran to and fro, dodging, hurling stones, and swearing in barbaric trebles.

From a window of an apartment-house that uprose from amid squat ignorant stables there leaned a curious woman. Some labourers, unloading a scow at a dock at the river, paused for a moment and regarded the fight. The engineer of a passive tugboat hung lazily over a railing and watched. Over on the island a worm of yellow convicts came from the shadow of a grey ominous building and crawled slowly along the river's bank.

A stone had smashed in Jimmie's mouth. Blood was bubbling over his chin and down upon his ragged shirt. Tears made furrows on his dirt-stained cheeks. His thin legs had begun to tremble and turn weak, causing his small body to reel. His roaring curses of the first part of the fight had changed to a blasphemous chatter.

In the yells of the whirling mob of Devil's Row children there were notes of joy like songs of triumphant savagery. The little boys seemed to leer gloatingly at the blood upon the other child's face.

Down the avenue came boastfully sauntering a lad of sixteen years, although the chronic sneer of an ideal manhood already sat upon his lips. His hat was tipped over his eye with an air of challenge. Between his teeth a cigar stump was tilted at the angle of defiance. He walked with a certain swing of the shoulders which appalled the timid. He glanced over into the vacant lot in which the little raving boys from Devil's Row seethed about the shrieking and tearful child from Rum Alley.

'Gee!' he murmured with interest, 'a scrap. Gee!'

He strode over to the cursing circle, swinging his shoulders in a manner which denoted that he held victory in his fists. He approached at the back of one of the most deeply engaged of the Devil's Row children.

'Ah, what d' hell,' he said, and smote the deeply engaged one on the back of the head. The little boy fell to the ground and gave a tremendous howl. He scrambled to his feet, and perceiving, evidently, the size of his assailant, ran quickly off, shouting alarms. The entire Devil's Row party followed him. They came to a stand a short distance away and yelled taunting oaths at the boy with the chronic sneer. The latter, momentarily, paid no attention to them.

'What's wrong wi'che, Jimmie?' he asked of the small champion.

Jimmie wiped his blood-wet features with his sleeve.

'Well, it was dis way, Pete, see! I was goin' teh lick dat Riley kid and dey all pitched on me.'

Some Rum Alley children now came forward. The party stood for a moment exchanging vainglorious remarks with Devil's Row. A few stones were thrown at long distances, and words of challenge passed between small warriors. Then the Rum Alley contingent turned slowly in the direction of their home street. They began to give, each to each, distorted versions of the fight. Causes of retreat in particular cases were magnified. Blows dealt in the fight were enlarged to catapultian power, and stones thrown were alleged to have hurtled with infinite accuracy. Valour grew strong again, and the little boys began to brag with great spirit.

'Ah, we blokies kin lick d' hull d—n Row,' said a child, swaggering.

Little Jimmie was trying to stanch the flow of blood from his cut lips. Scowling, he turned upon the speaker.

'Ah, where was yehs when I was doin' all deh fightin'?' he demanded. 'Youse kids makes me tired.'

'Ah, go ahn!' replied the other argumentatively.

Jimmie replied with heavy contempt. 'Ah, youse can't fight, Blue Billie! I kin lick yeh wid one han'.'

'Ah, go ahn!' replied Billie again.

'Ah!' said Jimmie threateningly.

'Ah!' said the other in the same tone.

They struck at each other, clinched, and rolled over on the cobblestones.

'Smash 'im, Jimmie, kick d' face off 'im!' yelled Pete, the lad with the chronic sneer, in tones of delight.

The small combatants pounded and kicked, scratched and tore. They began to weep and their curses struggled in their throats with sobs. The other little boys clasped their hands and wriggled their legs in **excitement**. They formed a bobbing circle about the pair.

A tiny spectator was suddenly agitated.

'Cheese it, Jimmie, cheese it! Here comes yer fader,' he yelled.

The circle of little boys instantly parted. They drew away and waited in ecstatic awe for that which was about to happen. The two little boys, fighting in the modes of four thousand years ago, did not hear the warning.

Up the avenue there plodded slowly a man with sullen eyes. He was carrying a dinner-pail and smoking an apple-wood pipe.

As he neared the spot where the little boys strove, he regarded them listlessly. But suddenly he roared an oath and advanced upon the rolling fighters.

'Here, you Jim, git up, now, while I belt yer life out, yeh disorderly brat.'

He began to kick into the chaotic mass on the ground. The boy Billie felt a heavy boot strike his head. He made a furious effort and disentangled himself from Jimmie. He tottered away.

Jimmie arose painfully from the ground and confronting his father began to curse him. His parent kicked him. 'Come home, now,' he cried, 'an' stop yer jawin', er I'll lam the everlasting head off yehs.'

They departed. The man paced placidly along with the apple-wood emblem of serenity between his teeth. The boy followed a dozen feet in the rear. He swore luridly, for he felt that it was degradation for one who aimed to be some vague kind of a soldier, or a man of blood with a sort of sublime license, to be taken home by a father.

CHAPTER 2

Eventually they entered a dark region where, from a careening building, a dozen gruesome doorways gave up loads of babies to the street and the gutter. A wind of early autumn raised yellow dust from cobbles and swirled it against a hundred windows. Long streamers of garments fluttered from fire-escapes. In all unhandy places there were buckets, brooms, rags and bottles. In the street infants played or fought with other infants or sat stupidly in the way of vehicles. Formidable women, with uncombed hair and disordered dress, gossiped while leaning on railings, or screamed in frantic quarrels. Withered persons, in curious postures of submission to something, sat smoking pipes in obscure corners. A thousand odours of cooking food came forth to the street. The building quivered and creaked from the weight of humanity stamping about in its bowels.

A small ragged girl dragged a red, bawling infant along the crowded ways. He was hanging back, baby-like, bracing his wrinkled, bare legs.

The little girl cried out: 'Ah, Tommie, come ahn. Dere's Jimmie and fader. Don't be a-pullin' me back.'

She jerked the baby's arm impatiently. He fell on his face, roaring. With a second jerk she pulled him to his feet, and they went on. With the obstinacy of his order, he protested against being dragged in a chosen direction. He made heroic endeavours to keep on his legs, denounced his sister, and consumed a bit of orange-peeling which he chewed between times of his infantile orations.

As the sullen-eyed man, followed by the blood-covered boy, drew near the little girl burst into reproachful cries. 'Ah, Jimmie, youse bin fightin' agin.'

The urchin swelled disdainfully.

'Ah, what d' hell, Mag. See?'

The little girl upbraided him. 'You'se allus fightin', Jimmie, an' yeh knows it puts mudder out when yehs come home half dead, an' it's like we'll all get a poundin'.'

She began to weep. The babe threw back his head and roared at his prospects.

'Ah,' cried Jimmie, 'shut up er I'll smack yer mout'. See?'

As his sister continued her lamentations, he suddenly struck her. The little girl reeled, and, recovering herself, burst into tears and quaveringly cursed him. As she slowly retreated, her brother advanced, dealing her cuffs. The father heard, and turned about.

'Stop that, Jim, d'yeh hear? Leave yer sister alone on the street. It's like I can never beat any sense into yer wooden head.'

The urchin raised his voice in defiance to his parent, and continued his attacks. The babe bawled tremendously, protesting with great violence. During his sister's hasty manoeuvres he was dragged by the arm.

Finally the procession plunged into one of the gruesome doorways. They crawled up dark stairways and along cold, gloomy halls. At last the father pushed open a door, and they entered a lighted room in which a large woman was rampant.

She stopped in a career from a seething stove to a pan-covered table. As the father and children filed in she peered at them.

'Eh, what? Been fightin' agin!' She threw herself upon Jimmie. The urchin tried to dart behind the others, and in the scuffle the babe, Tommie, was knocked down. He protested with his usual vehemence because they had bruised his tender shins against a table leg.

The mother's massive shoulders heaved with anger. Grasping the urchin by the neck and shoulder she shook

6

him until he rattled. She dragged him to an unholy sink, and, soaking a rag in water, began to scrub his lacerated face with it. Jimmie screamed in pain, and tried to twist his shoulders out of the clasp of the huge arms.

The babe sat on the floor watching the scene, his face in contortions like that of a woman at a tragedy. The father, with a newly ladened pipe in his mouth, sat in a backless chair near the stove. Jimmie's cries annoyed him. He turned about and bellowed at his wife:

'Let the kid alone for a minute, will yeh, Mary? Yer allus poundin' 'im. When I come nights I can't get no rest 'cause yer allus poundin' a kid. Let up, d'yeh hear? Don't be allus poundin' a kid.'

The woman's operations on the urchin instantly increased in violence. At last she tossed him to a corner, where he limply lay weeping.

The wife put her immense hands on her hips, and with a chieftainlike stride approached her husband.

'Ho!' she said, with a great grunt of contempt. 'An' what in the devil are you stickin' your nose for?'

The babe crawled under the table, and, turning, peered out cautiously. The ragged girl retreated, and the urchin in the corner drew his legs carefully beneath him.

The man puffed his pipe calmly and put his great muddied boots on the back part of the stove.

'Go t' hell,' he said tranquilly.

The woman screamed, and shook her fists before her husband's eyes. The rough yellow of her face and neck flared suddenly crimson. She began to howl.

He puffed imperturbably at his pipe for a time, but finally arose and went to look out of the window into the darkening chaos of back yards.

'You've been drinkin', Mary,' he said. 'You'd better let up on the bot', ol' woman, or you'll git done.'

'You're a liar. I ain't had a drop,' she roared in reply. They had a lurid altercation.

The babe was staring out from under the table, his small face working in his excitement. The ragged girl went stealthily over to the corner where the urchin lay.

'Are yehs hurted much, Jimmie?' she whispered timidly.

'Not a little bit. See!' growled the little boy.

'Will I wash d' blood?'

'Naw!'

'Will I—'

'When I catch dat Riley kid I'll break 'is face! Dat's right! See?'

He turned his face to the wall as if resolved grimly to bide his time.

In the quarrel between husband and wife the woman was victor. The man seized his hat and rushed from the room, apparently determined upon a vengeful drunk. She followed to the door and thundered at him as he made his way downstairs.

She returned and stirred up the room until her children were bobbing about like bubbles.

'Git outa d' way,' she bawled persistently, waving feet with their dishevelled shoes near the heads of her children. She shrouded herself, puffing and snorting, in a cloud of steam at the stove, and eventually extracted a frying-pan full of potatoes that hissed.

She flourished it. 'Come t' yer suppers, now,' she cried with sudden exasperation. 'Hurry up, now, er I'll help yeh!'

The children scrambled hastily. With prodigious clatter they arranged themselves at table. The babe sat with his feet dangling high from a precarious infant's chair and gorged his small stomach. Jimmie forced, with feverish rapidity, the great-enveloped pieces between his wounded lips. Maggie, with side glances of fear of interruption, ate like a small pursued tigress.

The mother sat blinking at them. She delivered re-

8

proaches, swallowed potatoes, and drank from a yellow-brown bottle. After a time her mood changed, and she wept as she carried little Tommie into another room and laid him to sleep, with his fists doubled, in an old quilt of faded red and green grandeur. Then she came and moaned by the stove. She rocked to and fro upon a chair, shedding tears and crooning miserably to the two children about their 'poor mother' and 'yer fader, damn 'is soul.'

The little girl plodded between the table and the chair with a dish pan on it. She tottered on her small legs beneath burdens of dishes.

Jimmie sat nursing his various wounds. He cast furtive glances at his mother. His practised eye perceived her gradually emerge from a mist of muddled sentiment until her brain burned in drunken heat. He sat breathless.

Maggie broke a plate.

The mother started to her feet as if propelled.

'Good Gawd!' she howled. Her glittering eyes fastened on her child with sudden hatred. The fervent red of her face turned almost to purple. The little boy ran to the halls, shrieking like a monk in an earthquake.

He floundered about in darkness until he found the stairs. He stumbled, panic-stricken, to the next floor. An old woman opened a door. A light behind her threw a flare on the urchin's face.

'Eh, child, what is it dis time? Is yer fader beatin' yer mudder, or yer mudder beatin' yer fader?'

JIMMIE and the old woman listened along in the hall. Above the muffled roar of conversation, the dismal wailings of babies at night, the thumping of feet in unseen corridors and rooms, and the sound of varied hoarse shoutings in the street and the rattling of wheels over cobbles, they heard the screams of the child and the roars of the mother die away to a feeble moaning and a subdued bass muttering.

The old woman was a gnarled and leathery personage who could don at will an expression of great virtue. She possessed a small music-box capable of one tune, and a collection of 'God bless yehs' pitched in assorted keys of fervency. Each day she took a position upon the stones of Fifth Avenue, where she crooked her legs under her and crouched, immovable and hideous, like an idol. She received daily a small sum in pennies. It was contributed, for the most part, by persons who did not make their homes in that vicinity.

Once, when a lady had dropped her purse on the sidewalk, the gnarled woman had grabbed it and smuggled it with great dexterity beneath her cloak. When she was arrested she had cursed the lady into a partial swoon, and with her aged limbs, twisted from rheumatism, had kicked the breath out of a huge policeman whose conduct upon that occasion she referred to when she said, 'The police, d—n 'em!'

'Eh, Jimmie, it's a shame,' she said. 'Go, now, like a dear, an' buy me a can, an' if yer mudder raises 'ell all night yehs can sleep here.'

Jimmie took a tendered tin pail and seven pennies and departed. He passed into the side door of a saloon and went to the bar. Straining up on his toes he raised the pail and pennies as high as his arms would let him. He saw two hands thrust down to take them. Directly the same hands let down the filled pail, and he left.

In front of the gruesome doorway he met a lurching figure. It was his father, swaying about on uncertain legs.

'Give me deh can. See?' said the man.

'Ah, come off! I got dis can fer dat ol' woman, an' it 'ud be dirt teh swipe it. See?' cried Jimmie.

The father wrenched the pail from the urchin. He grasped it in both hands and lifted it to his mouth. He glued his lips to the under edge and tilted his head. His throat swelled until it seemed to grow near his chin. There was a tremendous gulping movement and the beer was gone.

The man caught his breath and laughed. He hit his son on the head with the empty pail. As it rolled clanging into the street, Jimmie began to scream, and kicked repeatedly at his father's shins.

'Look at deh dirt what yeh done me,' he yelled. 'Deh ol' woman 'ill be trowin' fits.'

He retreated to the middle of the street, but the old man did not pursue. He staggered towards the door.

'I'll paste yeh when I ketch yeh!' he shouted, and disappeared.

During the evening he had been standing against a bar drinking whiskies, and declaring to all comers confidentially: 'My home reg'lar livin' hell! Why do I come an' drin' whisk' here thish way? 'Cause home reg'lar livin' hell!'

Jimmie waited a long time in the street and then crept warily up through the building. He passed with great caution the door of the gnarled woman, and finally stopped outside his home and listened.

He could hear his mother moving heavily about among the furniture of the room. She was chanting in a mournful voice, occasionally interjecting bursts of volcanic wrath at the father, who, Jimmie judged, had sunk down on the floor or in a corner.

'Why deh blazes don' chere try teh keep Jim from fightin'? I'll break yer jaw!' she suddenly bellowed.

The man mumbled with drunken indifference. 'Ah, w'ats bitin' yeh? W'a's odds? W'a' makes kick?'

'Because he tears 'is clothes, yeh fool!' cried the woman in supreme wrath.

The husband seemed to become aroused. 'Go chase yerself!' he thundered fiercely in reply. There was a crash against the door and something broke into clattering fragments. Jimmie partially suppressed a yell and darted down the stairway. Below he paused and listened. He heard howls and curses, groans and shrieks—a confused chorus as if a battle were raging. With it all there was the crash of splintering furniture. The eyes of the urchin glared in his fear that one of them would discover him.

Curious faces appeared in doorways, and whispered comments passed to and fro. 'Ol' Johnson's playin' horse again.'

Jimmie stood until the noises ceased and the other inhabitants of the tenement had all yawned and shut their doors. Then he crawled upstairs with the caution of an invader of a panther's den. Sounds of laboured breathing came through the broken door panels. He pushed the door open and entered, quaking.

A glow from the fire threw red hues over the bare floor, the cracked and soiled plastering, and the overturned and broken furniture.

In the middle of the floor lay his mother asleep. In one corner of the room his father's limp body hung across the seat of a chair.

The urchin stole forward. He began to shiver in dread of awakening his parents. His mother's great chest was heaving painfully. Jimmie paused and looked down at her. Her face was inflamed and swollen from drinking. Her yellow brows shaded eyelids that had grown blue. Her tangled hair tossed in waves over her forehead. Her mouth was set in the same lines of vindictive hatred that it had, perhaps, borne during the fight. Her bare, red arms were thrown out above her head in an attitude of exhaustion, something, mayhap, like that of a sated villain.

The urchin bent over his mother. He was fearful lest she should open her eyes, and the dread within him was so strong that he could not forbear to stare, but hung as if fascinated over the woman's grim face. Suddenly her eyes opened. The urchin found himself looking straight into an expression, which, it would seem, had the power to change his blood to salt. He howled piercingly and fell backward.

The woman floundered for a moment, tossed her arms about her head as if in combat, and again began to snore.

Jimmie crawled back into the shadows and waited. A noise in the next room had followed his cry at the discovery that his mother was awake. He grovelled in the gloom, his eyes riveted upon the intervening door.

He heard it creak, and then the sound of a small voice came to him. 'Jimmie! Jimmie! Are yehs dere?' it whispered. The urchin started. The thin, white face of his sister looked at him from the doorway of the other room. She crept to him across the floor.

The father had not moved, but lay in the same death-like sleep. The mother writhed in an uneasy slumber, her chest wheezing as if she were in the agonies of strangulation. Out at the window a florid moon was peering over dark roofs, and in the distance the waters of a river glimmered pallidly.

The small frame of the ragged girl was quivering. Her features were haggard from weeping, and her eyes gleamed with fear. She grasped the urchin's arm in her little trembling hands and they huddled in a corner. The eyes of both were drawn, by some force, to stare at the woman's face, for they thought she need only to awake and all the fiends would come from below.

They crouched until the ghost mists of dawn appeared at the window, drawing close to the panes, and looking in at the prostrate, heaving body of the mother.

CHAPTER 4

THE babe, Tommie, died. He went away in an insignificant coffin, his small waxen hand clutching a flower that the girl, Maggie, had stolen from an Italian.

She and Jimmie lived.

The inexperienced fibres of the boy's eyes were hardened at an early age. He became a young man of leather. He lived some red years without labouring. During that time his sneer became chronic. He studied human nature in the gutter, and found it no worse than he thought he had reason to believe it. He never conceived a respect for the world, because he had begun with no idols that it had smashed.

He clad his soul in armour by means of happening hilariously in at a mission church where a man composed his sermons of 'you's'. Once a philosopher asked this man why he did not say 'we' instead of 'you'. The man replied, 'What?'

While they got warm at the stove he told his hearers just where he calculated they stood with the Lord. Many of the sinners were impatient over the pictured depths of their degradation. They were waiting for soup-tickets.

A reader of the words of wind demons might have been able to see the portions of a dialogue pass to and fro between the exhorter and his hearers.

'You are damned,' said the preacher. And the reader of sounds might have seen the reply go forth from the ragged people: 'Where's our soup?'

Jimmie and a companion sat in a rear seat and commented upon the things that didn't concern them, with all the freedom of English tourists. When they grew thirsty and went out, their minds confused the speaker with Christ.

Momentarily, Jimmie was sullen with thoughts of a hopeless altitude where grew fruit. His companion said that if he should ever go to heaven he would ask for a million dollars and a bottle of beer.

Jimmie's occupation for a long time was to stand at street corners and watch the world go by, dreaming blood-red dreams at the passing of pretty women. He menaced mankind at the intersections of streets.

At the corners he was in life and of life. The world was going on and he was there to perceive it.

He maintained a belligerent attitude towards all well-dressed men. To him fine raiment was allied to weakness, and all good coats covered faint hearts. He and his orders were kings, to a certain extent, over the men of un-tarnished clothes, because these latter dreaded, perhaps, to be either killed or laughed at.

Above all things he despised obvious Christians and ciphers with the chrysanthemums of aristocracy in their button-holes. He considered himself above both of these classes. He was afraid of nothing.

When he had a dollar in his pocket his satisfaction with existence was the greatest thing in the world. So, event-ually, he felt obliged to work. His father died and his mother's years were divided up into periods of thirty days.

He became a truck-driver. There was given to him the charge of a painstaking pair of horses and a large rattling truck. He invaded the turmoil and tumble of the down-town streets, and learned to breathe maledictory defiance at the police, who occasionally used to climb up, drag him from his perch, and punch him.

In the lower part of the city he daily involved himself in hideous tangles. If he and his team chanced to be in the rear he preserved a demeanour of serenity, crossing his legs and bursting forth into yells when foot passengers took dangerous dives beneath the noses of his champing horses. He smoked his pipe calmly, for he knew that his pay was marching on.

If his charge was in the front, and if it became the key-truck of chaos, he entered terrifically into the quarrel that was raging to and fro among the drivers on their high seats, and sometimes roared oaths and violently got himself arrested.

After a time his sneer grew so that it turned its glare upon all things. He became so sharp that he believed in nothing. To him the police were always actuated by malignant impulses, and the rest of the world was composed, for the most part, of despicable creatures who were all trying to take advantage of him, and with whom, in defence, he was obliged to quarrel on all possible occasions. He himself occupied a downtrodden position, which had a private but distinct element of grandeur in its isolation.

The greatest cases of aggravated idiocy were, to his mind, rampant upon the front platforms of all of the street cars. At first his tongue strove with these beings, but he eventually became superior. In him grew a majestic contempt for those strings of street cars that followed him like intent bugs.

He fell into the habit, when starting on a long journey, of fixing his eye on a high and distant object, commanding his horses to start and then going into a trance of observation. Multitudes of drivers might howl in his rear, and passengers might load him with opprobrium, but he would not awaken until some blue policeman turned red and began frenziedly to seize bridles and beat the soft noses of the responsible horses.

When he paused to contemplate the attitude of the police towards himself and his fellows, he believed that they were the only men in the city who had no rights. When driving about he felt that he was held liable by the police for anything that might occur in the streets, and that he was the common prey of all energetic officials. In revenge, he resolved never to move out of the way of anything, until formidable circumstances or a much larger man than himself forced him to it.

Foot passengers were mere pestering flies with an insane disregard for their legs and his convenience. He could not comprehend their desire to cross the streets. Their madness smote him with eternal amazement. He was continually storming at them from his throne. He sat aloft and denounced their frantic leaps, plunges, dives, and straddles.

When they would thrust at, or parry, the noses of his champing horses, making them swing their heads and move their feet, and thus disturbing a stolid, dreamy repose, he swore at the men as fools, for he himself could perceive that Providence had caused it clearly to be written that he and his team had the unalienable right to stand in the proper path of the sun chariot, and if they so minded, to obstruct its mission or take a wheel off.

And if the god driver had had a desire to step down, put up his flame-coloured fists, and manfully dispute the right of way, he would have probably been immediately opposed by a scowling mortal with two sets of hard knuckles.

It is possible, perhaps, that this young man would have derided, in an axle-wide alley, the approach of a flying ferry-boat. Yet he achieved a respect for a fire-engine. As one charged towards his truck, he would drive fearfully upon a sidewalk, threatening untold people with annihilation. When an engine struck a mass of blocked trucks, splitting it into fragments, as a blow annihilates a cake of ice, Jimmie's team could usually be observed high and safe, with whole wheels, on the sidewalk. The fearful coming of the engine could break up the most intricate muddle of heavy vehicles at which the police had been storming for half an hour.

A fire-engine was enshrined in his heart as an appalling thing that he loved with a distant, dog-like devotion. It had been known to overturn a street car. Those leaping horses, striking sparks from the cobbles in their forward lunge, were creatures to be ineffably admired. The clang of the gong pierced his breast like a noise of remembered war.

When Jimmie was a little boy he began to be arrested. Before he reached a great age, he had a fair record.

He developed too great a tendency to climb down from his truck and fight with other drivers. He had been in quite a number of miscellaneous fights, and in some general bar-room rows that had become known to the police. Once he had been arrested for assaulting a China-man. Two women in different parts of the city, and entirely unknown to each other, caused him considerable annoyance by breaking forth simultaneously, at fateful intervals, into wailings about marriage and support and infants.

Nevertheless, he had, on a certain star-lit evening, said wonderingly and quite reverently 'Deh moon looks like hell, don't it?'

THE girl, Maggie, blossomed in a mud puddle. She grew to be a most rare and wonderful production of a tenement district, a pretty girl.

None of the dirt of Rum Alley seemed to be in her veins. The philosophers upstairs, downstairs, and on the same floor, puzzled over it.

When a child, playing and fighting with gamins in the street, dirt disgusted her. Attired in tatters and grime, she went unseen.

There came a time, however, when the young men of the vicinity said, 'Dat Johnson goil is a putty good looker.' About this period her brother remarked to her: 'Mag, I'll tell yeh dis! See? Yeh've eeder got t' go on d' toif er go t' work!' Whereupon she went to work, having the feminine aversion to the alternative.

By a chance, she got a position in an establishment where they made collars and cuffs. She received a stool and a machine in a room where sat twenty girls of various shades of yellow discontent. She perched on the stool and treadled at her machine all day, turning out collars with a name which might have been noted for its irrelevancy to anything with collars. At night she returned home to her mother.

Jimmie grew large enough to take the vague position of head of the family. As incumbent of that office, he stumbled upstairs late at night, as his father had done before him. He reeled about the room, swearing at his relations, or went to sleep on the floor.

The mother had gradually arisen to such a degree of fame that she could bandy words with her acquaintances among the police justices. Court officials called her by her first name. When she appeared they pursued a course which had been theirs for months. They invariably grinned, and cried out, 'Hello, Mary, you here again?' Her grey head wagged in many courts. She always besieged the bench with voluble excuses, explanations, apologies, and prayers. Her flaming face and rolling eyes were a familiar sight on the island. She measured time by means of sprees, and was swollen and dishevelled.

One day the young man Pete, who as a lad had smitten the Devil's Row urchin in the back of the head and put to flight the antagonists of his friend Jimmie, strutted upon the scene. He met Jimmie one day on the street, promised to take him to a boxing match in Williamsburg, and called for him in the evening.

Maggie observed Pete.

He sat on a table in the Johnson home, and dangled his checked legs with an enticing nonchalance. His hair was curled down over his forehead in an oiled bang. His pugged nose seemed to revolt from contact with a bristling moustache of short, wire-like hairs. His blue, double-breasted coat, edged with black braid, was buttoned close to a red puff tie, and his patent leather shoes looked like weapons.

His mannerisms stamped him as a man who had a correct sense of his personal superiority. There were valour and contempt for circumstances in the glance of his eye. He waved his hands like a man of the world who dismisses religion and philosophy, and says, 'Rats!' He had certainly seen everything, and with each curl of his lip he declared that it amounted to nothing. Maggie thought he must be a very 'elegant' bar-tender.

He was telling tales to Jimmie.

Maggie watched him furtively, with half-closed eyes, lit with a vague interest.

'Hully gee! Dey makes me tired,' he said. 'Mos' e'ry day some farmer comes in an' tries t' run d' shop. See?

But d' gits t'rowed right out. I jolt dem right out in d' street before dey knows where dey is. See?'

'Sure,' said Jimmie.

'Dere was a mug come in d' place d' odder day wid an idear he wus goin' t' own d' place. Hully gee! he wus goin' t' own d' place. I see he had a still on, an' I didn' wanna giv 'im no stuff, so I says, "Git outa here an' don' make no trouble," I says like dat. See? "Git outa here an' don' make no trouble;" like dat. "Git outa here," I says. See?'

Jimmie nodded understandingly. Over his features played an eager desire to state the amount of his valour in a similar crisis, but the narrator proceeded.

'Well, deh blokie he says: "'T' blazes wid it! I ain' lookin' for no scrap," he says—see? "but," he says, "I'm 'spectable cit'zen an' I wanna drink, an' quick, too." See? "Aw, goahn!" I says, like dat. "Aw, goahn," I says See? "Don' make no trouble," I says, like dat. "Don' make no trouble." See? Den d' mug he squared off an' said he was fine as silk wid his dukes—see? an' he wan'ed a drink—quick. Dat's what he said. See?'

'Sure,' repeated Jimmie.

Pete continued. 'Say, I jes' jumped d' bar, an' d' way I plunked dat blokie was outa sight. See? Dat's right! In d' jaw! See? Hully gee! he t'rowed a spittoon true d' front windee. Say, I taut I'd drop dead. But d' boss, he comes in after, an' he says: "Pete, yehs done jes' right! Yeh've gota keep order, an' it's all right." See? "It's all right," he says. Dat's what he said.'

The two held a technical discussion.

'Dat bloke was a dandy,' said Pete, in conclusion, 'but he hadn' oughta made no trouble. Dat's what I says t' dem: "Don' come in here an' make no trouble," I says, like dat. "Don' make no trouble." See?'

As Jimmie and his friend exchanged tales descriptive of their prowess, Maggie leaned back in the shadow. Her eyes dwelt wonderingly and rather wistfully upon Pete's face. The broken furniture, grimy walls, and general disorder and dirt of her home of a sudden appeared before her and began to take a potential aspect. Pete's aristocratic person looked as if it might soil. She looked keenly at him, occasionally wondering if he was feeling contempt. But Pete seemed to be enveloped in reminiscence.

'Hully gee!' said he, 'dose mugs can't feaze me. Dey knows I kin wipe up d' street wid any tree of dem.'

When he said, 'Ah, what d' hell!' his voice was burdened with disdain for the inevitable and contempt for anything that fate might compel him to endure.

Maggie perceived that here was the ideal man. Her dim thoughts were often searching for far-away lands where the little hills sing together in the morning. Under the trees of her dream-gardens there had always walked a lover.

CHAPTER 6

PETE took note of Maggie.

'Say, Mag, I'm stuck on yer shape. It's outa sight,' he said parenthetically, with an affable grin.

As he became aware that she was listening closely, he grew still more eloquent in his description of various happenings in his career. It appeared that he was invincible in fights.

'Why,' he said, referring to a man with whom he had had a misunderstanding, 'dat mug scrapped like a dago. Dat's right. He was dead easy. See? He taut he was a scrapper. But he foun' out diff'ent. Hully gee!'

He walked to and fro in the small room, which seemed then to grow even smaller and unfit to hold his dignity, the attribute of a supreme warrior. That swing of the shoulders which had frozen the timid when he was but a lad had increased with his growth and education in the ratio of ten to one. It, combined with the sneer upon his mouth, told mankind that there was nothing in space which could appal him. Maggie marvelled at him and surrounded him with greatness. She vaguely tried to calculate the altitude of the pinnacle from which he must have looked down upon her.

'I met a chump deh odder day way up in deh city,' he said. 'I was goin' teh see a frien' of mine. When I was a-crossin' deh street deh chump runned plump inteh me, an' den he turns aroun' an' says, "Yer insolen' ruffin!" he says, like dat. "Oh, gee!" I says, "oh, gee! git off d' eart'!" I says, like dat. See? "Git off d' eart'!" like dat. Den deh blokie he got wild. He says I was a contempt'ble scoun'el, er somethin' like dat, an' he says I was doom' teh everlastin' pe'dition, er somethin' like dat. "Gee!" I says,

—"gee! Yer joshin' me," I says. "Yer joshin' me." An' den I slugged 'im. See?"

With Jimmie in his company, Pete departed in a sort of blaze of glory from the Johnson home. Maggie, leaning from the window, watched him as he walked down the street.

Here was a formidable man who disdained the strength of a world full of fists. Here was one who had contempt for brass-clothed power; one whose knuckles could ring defiantly against the granite of law. He was a knight.

The two men went from under the glimmering street lamp and passed into shadows.

Turning, Maggie contemplated the dark, dust-stained walls, and the scant and crude furniture of her home. A clock, in a splintered and battered oblong box of varnished wood, she suddenly regarded as an abomination. She noted that it ticked raspingly. The almost vanished flowers in the carpet pattern, she conceived to be newly hideous. Some faint attempts which she had made with blue ribbon to freshen the appearance of a dingy curtain, she now saw to be piteous.

She wondered what Pete dined on.

She reflected upon the collar-and-cuff factory. It began to appear to her mind as a dreary place of endless grinding. Pete's elegant occupation brought him, no doubt, into contact with people who had money and manners. It was probable that he had a large acquaintance with pretty girls. He must have great sums of money to spend.

To her the earth was composed of hardships and insults. She felt instant admiration for a man who openly defied it. She thought that if the grim angel of death should clutch his heart, Pete would shrug his shoulders and say, 'Oh, ev'ryt'ing goes.'

She anticipated that he would come again shortly. She spent some of her week's pay in the purchase of flowered cretonne for a lambrequin. She made it with infinite care,

24

and hung it to the slightly careening mantel over the stove in the kitchen. She studied it with painful anxiety from different points in the room. She wanted it to look well on Sunday night when, perhaps, Jimmie's friend would come. On Sunday night, however, Pete did not appear.

Afterwards the girl looked at it with a sense of humiliation. She was now convinced that Pete was superior to admiration for lambrequins.

A few evenings later Pete entered with fascinating innovations in his apparel. As she had seen him twice and he wore a different suit each time, Maggie had a dim impression that his wardrobe was prodigious.

'Say, Mag,' he said, 'put on yer bes' duds Friday night an' I'll take yehs t' d' show. See?'

He spent a few moments in flourishing his clothes, and then vanished without having glanced at the lambrequin.

Over the eternal collars and cuffs in the factory Maggie spent the most of three days in making imaginary sketches of Pete and his daily environment. She imagined some half-dozen women in love with him, and thought he must lean dangerously towards an indefinite one, whom she pictured as endowed with great charms of person, but with an altogether contemptible disposition.

She thought he must live in a blare of pleasure. He had friends and people who were afraid of him.

She saw the golden glitter of the place where Pete was to take her. It would be an entertainment of many hues and many melodies, where she was afraid she might appear small and mouse-coloured.

Her mother drank whisky all Friday morning. With lurid face and tossing hair she cursed and destroyed furniture all Friday afternoon. When Maggie came home at half past six her mother lay asleep amid the wreck of chairs and a table. Fragments of various household utensils were scattered about the floor. She had vented some phase of drunken fury upon the lambrequin. It lay in a bedraggled heap in the corner.

'Hah!' she snorted, sitting up suddenly, 'where yeh been? Why don' yeh come home earlier? Been loafin' 'round d' streets. Yer gettin' t' be a reg'lar devil.'

When Pete arrived, Maggie, in a worn black dress, was waiting for him in the midst of a floor strewn with wreckage. The curtain at the window had been pulled by a heavy hand and hung by one tack, dangling to and fro in the draught through the cracks at the sash. The knots of blue ribbon appeared like violated flowers. The fire in the stove had gone out. The displaced lids and open doors showed heaps of sullen grey ashes. The remnants of a meal, ghastly, lay in a corner. Maggie's mother, stretched on the floor, blasphemed, and gave her daughter a bad name.

CHAPTER 7

An orchestra of yellow silk women and bald-headed men, on an elevated stage near the centre of a great green-hued ball, played a popular waltz. The place was crowded with people grouped about little tables. A battalion of waiters slid among the throng, carrying trays of beer-glasses, and making change from the inexhaustible vaults of their trousers pockets. Little boys, in the costumes of French chefs, paraded up and down the irregular aisles vending fancy cakes. There was a low rumble of conversation and a subdued clinking of glasses. Clouds of tobacco smoke rolled and wavered high in air above the dull gilt of the chandeliers.

The vast crowd had an air throughout of having just quitted labour. Men with calloused hands, and attired in garments that showed the wear of an endless drudging for a living, smoked their pipes contentedly and spent five, ten, or perhaps fifteen cents for beer. There was a mere sprinkling of men who smoked cigars purchased elsewhere. The great body of the crowd was composed of people who showed that all day they strove with their hands. Quiet Germans, with maybe their wives and two or three children, sat listening to the music, with the expressions of happy cows. An occasional party of sailors from a warship, their faces pictures of sturdy health, spent the earlier hours of the evening at the small round tables. Very infrequent tipsy men, swollen with the value of their opinions, engaged their companions in earnest and confidential conversation. In the balcony, and here and there below, shone the impassive faces of women. The nationalities of the Bowery beamed upon the stage from all directions.

Pete walked aggressively up a side aisle and took seats with Maggie at a table beneath the balcony.

'Two beehs!'

Leaning back, he regarded with eyes of superiority the scene before them. This attitude affected Maggie strongly. A man who could regard such a sight with indifference must be accustomed to very great things.

It was obvious that Pete had visited this place many times before, and was very familiar with it. A knowledge of this fact made Maggie feel little and new.

He was extremely gracious and attentive. He displayed the consideration of a cultured gentleman who knew what was due.

'Say, what's eatin' yeh? Bring d' lady a big glass! What use is dat pony?'

'Don't be fresh, now,' said the waiter, with some warmth, as he departed.

'Ah, git off d' eart!' said Pete, after the other's retreating form.

Maggie perceived that Pete brought forth all his elegance and all his knowledge of high-class customs for her benefit. Her heart warmed as she reflected upon his condescension.

The orchestra of yellow silk women and bald-headed men gave vent to a few bars of anticipatory music, and a girl, in a pink dress with short skirts, galloped upon the stage. She smiled upon the throng as if in acknowledgment of a warm welcome, and began to walk to and fro, making profuse gesticulations, and singing, in brazen soprano tones, a song the words of which were inaudible. When she broke into the swift rattling measures of a chorus some half-tipsy men near the stage joined in the rollicking refrain, and glasses were pounded rhythmically upon the tables. People leaned forward to watch her and to try to catch the words of the song. When she vanished there were long rollings of applause.

Obedient to more anticipatory bars, she reappeared among the half-suppressed cheering of the tipsy men. The orchestra plunged into dance music, and the laces of the dancer fluttered and flew in the glare of gas-jets. She divulged the fact that she was attired in some half-dozen skirts. It was patent that any one of them would have proved adequate for the purpose for which skirts are intended. An occasional man bent forward, intent upon the pink stockings. Maggie wondered at the splendour of the costume and lost herself in calculations of the cost of the silks and laces.

The dancer's smile of enthusiasm was turned for ten minutes upon the faces of her audience. In the finale she fell into some of those grotesque attitudes which were at the time popular among the dancers in the theatres up-town giving to the Bowery public the diversions of the aristocratic theatre-going public at reduced rates.

'Say, Pete,' said Maggie, leaning forward, 'dis is great.'

'Sure!' said Pete, with proper complacence.

A ventriloquist followed the dancer. He held two fantastic dolls on his knees. He made them sing mournful ditties and say funny things about geography and Ireland.

'Do dose little men talk?' asked Maggie.

'Naw,' said Pete, 'it's some big jolly. See?'

Two girls, set down on the bills as sisters, came forth and sang a duet which is heard occasionally at concerts given under church auspices. They supplemented it with a dance, which, of course, can never be seen at concerts given under church auspices.

After they had retired, a woman of debatable age sang a Negro melody. The chorus necessitated some grotesque waddlings supposed to be an imitation of a plantation darky, under the influence, probably, of music and the moon. The audience was just enthusiastic enough over it to make her return and sing a sorrowful lay, whose lines told of a mother's love, and a sweetheart who waited, and a young man who was lost at sea under harrowing circumstances. From the faces of a score or so in the crowd the self-contained look faded. Many heads were bent forward with eagerness and sympathy. As the last distressing sentiment of the piece was brought forth, it was greeted by the kind of applause which rings as sincere.

As a final effort, the singer rendered some verses which described a vision of Britain annihilated by America, and Ireland bursting her bonds. A carefully prepared climax was reached in the last line of the last verse, when the singer threw out her arms and cried, 'The star-spangled banner.' Instantly a great cheer swelled from the throats of this assemblage of the masses, most of them of foreign birth. There was a heavy rumble of booted feet thumping the floor. Eyes gleamed with sudden fire, and calloused hands waved frantically in the air.

After a few moments' rest, the orchestra played noisily, and a small, fat man burst out upon the stage. He began to roar a song and to stamp back and forth before the footlights, wildly waving a silk hat and throwing leers broadcast. He made his face into fantastic grimaces until he looked like a devil on a Japanese kite. The crowd laughed gleefully. His short, fat legs were never still a moment. He shouted and roared and bobbed his shock of red wig until the audience broke out in excited applause.

Pete did not pay much attention to the progress of events upon the stage. He was drinking beer and watching Maggie.

Her cheeks were blushing with excitement and her eyes were glistening. She drew deep breaths of pleasure. No thoughts of the atmosphere of the collar-and-cuff factory came to her.

With the final crash of the orchestra they jostled their way to the sidewalk in the crowd. Pete took Maggie's arm and pushed a way for her, offering to fight with a man or two. They reached Maggie's home at a late hour and stood for a moment in front of the gruesome doorway.

'Say, Mag,' said Pete, 'give us a kiss for takin' yeh t' d' show, will yer?'

Maggie laughed, as if startled, and drew away from him.

'Naw, Pete,' she said, 'dat wasn't in it.'

'Ah, why wasn't it?' urged Pete.

The girl retreated nervously.

'Ah, go ahn!' repeated he.

Maggie darted into the hall, and up the stairs. She turned and smiled at him, then disappeared.

Pete walked slowly down the street. He had something of an astonished expression upon his features. He paused under a lamp-post and breathed a low breath of surprise.

'Gee!' he said, 'I wonner if I've been played fer a duffer.'

As thoughts of Pete came to Maggie's mind, she began to have an intense dislike for all of her dresses.

'What ails yeh? What makes ye be allus fixin' and fussin'?' her mother would frequently roar at her.

She began to note with more interest the well-dressed women she met on the avenues. She envied elegance and soft palms. She craved those adornments of person which she saw every day on the street, conceiving them to be allies of vast importance to women.

Studying faces, she thought many of the women and girls she chanced to meet smiled with serenity as though for ever cherished and watched over by those they loved.

The air in the collar-and-cuff establishment strangled her. She knew she was gradually and surely shrivelling in the hot, stuffy room. The begrimed windows rattled incessantly from the passing of elevated trains. The place was filled with a whirl of noises and odours.

She became lost in thought as she looked at some of the grizzled women in the room, more mechanical contrivances sewing seams and grinding out, with heads bent over their work, tales of imagined or real girlhood happiness, or of past drunks, or the baby at home, and unpaid wages. She wondered how long her youth would endure. She began to see the bloom upon her cheeks as something of value.

She imagined herself, in an exasperating future, as a scrawny woman with an eternal grievance. She thought Pete to be a very fastidious person concerning the appearance of women.

She felt that she should love to see somebody entangle their fingers in the oily beard of the fat foreigner who owned the establishment. He was a detestable creature. He wore white socks with low shoes. He sat all day delivering orations in the depths of a cushioned chair. His pocket-book deprived them of the power of retort.

'What do you sink I pie fife dolla a week for? Play? No, py damn!'

Maggie was anxious for a friend to whom she could talk about Pete. She would have liked to discuss his admirable mannerisms with a reliable mutual friend. At home, she found her mother often drunk and always raving. It seemed that the world had treated this woman very badly, and she took a deep revenge upon such portions of it as came within her reach. She broke furniture as if she were at last getting her rights. She swelled with virtuous indignation as she carried the lighter articles of household use, one by one, under the shadows of the three gilt balls, where Hebrews chained them with chains of interest.

Jimmie came when he was obliged to by circumstances over which he had no control. His well-trained legs brought him staggering home, and put him to bed some nights when he would rather have gone elsewhere.

Swaggering Pete loomed like a golden sun to Maggie. He took her to a dime museum, where rows of meek freaks astonished her. She contemplated their deformities with awe, and thought them a sort of chosen tribe.

Pete, racking his brains for amusement, discovered the Central Park Menagerie and the Museum of Arts. Sunday afternoons would sometimes find them at these places. Pete did not appear to be particularly interested in what he saw. He stood around looking heavy, while Maggie giggled in glee.

Once at the menagerie he went into a trance of admiration before the spectacle of a very small monkey threatening to thrash a cageful because one of them had pulled his tail and he had not wheeled about quickly enough to discover who did it. Ever after Pete knew that monkey by sight, and winked at him, trying to induce him to fight with other and larger monkeys.

At the museum, Maggie said, 'Dis is outa sight!'

'Aw, rats!' said Pete; 'wait till next summer an' I'll take yehs to a picnic.'

While the girl wandered in the vaulted rooms, Pete occupied himself in returning stony stare for stony stare, the appalling scrutiny of the watchdogs of the treasures. Occasionally he would remark in loud tones, 'Dat jay has got glass eyes,' and sentences of the sort. When he tired of this amusement he would go to the mummies and moralize over them.

Usually he submitted with silent dignity to all that he had to go through, but at times he was goaded into comment.

'Aw!' he demanded once. 'Look at all dese little jugs! Hundred jugs in a row! Ten rows in a case, an' 'bout a t'ousand cases! What d' blazes use is dem?'

In the evenings of week days he often took her to see plays in which the dazzling heroine was rescued from the palatial home of her treacherous guardian by the hero with the beautiful sentiments. The latter spent most of his time out at soak in pale-green snowstorms, busy with a nickel-plated revolver rescuing aged strangers from villains.

Maggie lost herself in sympathy with the wanderers swooning in snowstorms beneath happy-hued church windows, while a choir within sang 'Joy to the World'. To Maggie and the rest of the audience this was trans-cendental realism. Joy always within, and they, like the actor, inevitably without. Viewing it, they hugged them-selves in ecstatic pity of their imagined or real condition.

The girl thought the arrogance and granite-heartedness of the magnate of the play were very accurately drawn. She echoed the maledictions that the occupants of the gallery showered on this individual when his lines com-pelled him to expose his extreme selfishness.

Shady persons in the audience revolted from the pictured villainy of the drama. With untiring zeal they hissed vice and applauded virtue. Unmistakably bad men evinced an apparently sincere admiration for virtue. The loud gallery was overwhelmingly with the unfortunate and the oppressed. They encouraged the struggling hero with cries, and jeered the villain, hooting and calling attention to his whiskers. When anybody died in the pale-green snowstorms, the gallery mourned. They sought out the painted misery and hugged it as akin.

In the hero's erratic march from poverty in the first act, to wealth and triumph in the final one, in which he forgives all the enemies that he has left, he was assisted by the gallery, which applauded his generous and noble sentiments and confounded the speeches of his opponents by making irrelevant but very sharp remarks. Those actors who were cursed with the parts of villains were confronted at every turn by the gallery. If one of them rendered lines containing the most subtle distinctions between right and wrong, the gallery was immediately aware that the actor meant wickedness, and denounced him accordingly.

The last act was a triumph for the hero, poor and of the masses, the representative of the audience, over the villain and the rich man, his pockets stuffed with bonds, his heart packed with tyrannical purposes, imperturbable amid suffering.

Maggie always departed with raised spirits from these melodramas. She rejoiced at the way in which the poor and virtuous eventually overcame the wealthy and wicked. The theatre made her think. She wondered if the culture and refinement she had seen imitated, perhaps grotesquely, by the heroine on the stage, could be acquired by a girl who lived in a tenement house and worked in a shirt factory.

CHAPTER 9

A GROUP of urchins were intent upon the side door of a saloon. Expectancy gleamed from their eyes. They were twisting their fingers in excitement.

'Here she comes!' yelled one of them suddenly.

The group of urchins burst instantly asunder and its individual fragments were spread in a wide, respectable half-circle about the point of interest. The saloon door opened with a crash, and the figure of a woman appeared upon the threshold. Her grey hair fell in knotted masses about her shoulders. Her face was crimsoned and wet with perspiration. Her eyes had a rolling glare.

'Not a cent more of me money will yehs ever get—not a red! I spent me money here fer t'ree years, an' now yehs tells me yeh'll sell me no more stuff! Go fall on yerself, Johnnie Murckre! "Disturbance?" Disturbance be blowed! Go fall on yerself, Johnnie—'

The door received a kick of exasperation from within, and the woman lurched heavily out on the sidewalk.

The gamins in the half circle became violently agitated. They began to dance about and hoot and yell and jeer. A wide dirty grin spread over each face.

The woman made a furious dash at a particularly outrageous cluster of little boys. They laughed delightedly, and scampered off a short distance, calling out to her over their shoulders. She stood tottering on the curbstone and thundered at them.

'Yeh devil's kids!' she howled, shaking her fists. The little boys whooped in glee. As she started up the street they fell in behind and marched uproariously. Occasionally she wheeled about and made charges on them. They ran nimbly out of reach and taunted her.

In the frame of a gruesome doorway she stood for a moment cursing them. Her hair straggled, giving her red features a look of insanity. Her great fists quivered as she shook them madly in the air.

The urchins made terrific noises until she turned and disappeared. Then they filed off quietly in the way they had come.

The woman floundered about in the lower hall of the tenement house, and finally stumbled up the stairs. On an upper hall a door was opened and a collection of heads peered curiously out, watching her. With a wrathful snort the woman confronted the door, but it was slammed hastily in her face and the key was turned.

She stood for a few minutes, delivering a frenzied challenge at the panels.

'Come out in deh hall, Mary Murphy, if yehs want a scrap! Come ahn! Yeh overgrown terrier, come ahn!'

She began to kick the door. She shrilly defied the universe to appear and do battle. Her cursing trebles brought heads from all doors save the one she threatened. Her eyes glared in every direction. The air was full of her tossing fists.

'Come ahn! deh hull gang of yehs, come ahn!' she roared at the spectators. An oath or two, cat-calls, jeers, and bits of facetious advice were given in reply. Missiles clattered about her feet.

'What's wrong wi' che?' said a voice in the gathered gloom, and Jimmie came forward. He carried a tin dinner-pail in his hand and under his arm a truckman's brown apron done in a bundle. 'What's wrong?' he demanded.

'Come out! all of yehs, come out,' his mother was howling. 'Come ahn an' I'll stamp yer faces true d' floor.'

'Shet yer face, an' come home, yeh old fool!' roared Jimmie at her. She strode up to him and twirled her fingers in his face. Her eyes were darting flames of unreasoning rage and her frame trembled with eagerness for a fight.

'An' who are youse? I ain't givin' a snap of me fingers fer youse!' she bawled at him. She turned her huge back in tremendous disdain and climbed the stairs to the next floor.

Jimmie followed, and at the top of the flight he seized his mother's arm and started to drag her towards the door of their room.

'Come home!' he gritted between his teeth.

'Take yer hands off me! Take yer hands off me!' shrieked his mother.

She raised her arm and whirled her great fist at her son's face. Jimmie dodged his head and the blow struck him in the back of the neck. 'Come home!' he gritted again. He threw out his left hand and writhed his fingers about her middle arm. The mother and the son began to sway and struggle like gladiators.

'Whoop!' said the Rum Alley tenement house. The hall filled with interested spectators.

'Hi, ol' lady, dat was a dandy!'

'T'ree t' one on d' red!'

'Ah, quit yer scrappin'!'

The door of the Johnson home opened and Maggie looked out. Jimmie made a supreme cursing effort and hurled his mother into the room. He quickly followed and closed the door. The Rum Alley tenement swore disappointedly and retired.

The mother slowly gathered herself up from the floor. Her eyes glittered menacingly upon her children.

'Here now,' said Jimmie, 'we've had enough of dis. Sit down, an' don' make no trouble.'

He grasped her arm, and twisting it, forced her into a creaking chair.

'Keep yer hands off me!' roared his mother again.

'Say, yeh ol' bat! Quit dat!' yelled Jimmie, madly.

Maggie shrieked and ran into the other room. To her there came the sound of a storm of crashes and curses. There was a great final thump and Jimmie's voice cried: 'Dere now! Stay still.'

Maggie opened the door now, and went warily out. 'Oh, Jimmie!'

He was leaning against the wall and swearing. Blood stood upon bruises on his knotty forearms where they had scraped against the floor or the walls in the scuffle. The mother lay screeching on the floor, the tears running down her furrowed face.

Maggie, standing in the middle of the room, gazed about her. The usual upheaval of the tables and chairs had taken place. Crockery was strewn broadcast in fragments. The stove had been disturbed on its legs, and now leaned idiotically to one side. A pail had been upset and water spread in all directions.

The door opened and Pete appeared. He shrugged his shoulders. 'Oh, gee!' he observed.

He walked over to Maggie and whispered in her ear: 'Ah, what d' hell, Mag? Come ahn and we'll have a outa sight time.'

The mother in the corner upreared her head and shook her tangled locks.

'Aw yer bote no good, needer of yehs,' she said, glowering at her daughter in the gloom. Her eyes seemed to burn balefully. 'Yeh've gone t' d' devil, Mag Johnson, yehs knows yehs have gone t' d' devil. Yer a disgrace t' yer people. An' now, git out an' go ahn wid dat doe-faced jude of yours. Go wid him, curse yeh, an' a good riddance. Go, an' see how yeh likes it.'

Maggie gazed long at her mother.

'Go now, an' see how yeh likes it. Git out. I won't have sech as youse in me house! Git out, d' yeh hear! Damn yeh, git out!'

The girl began to tremble.

39

At this instant Pete came forward. 'Oh, what d' hell, Mag, see,' whispered he softly in her ear. 'Dis all blows over. See? D' ol' woman 'ill be all right in d' mornin'. Come ahn out wid me! We'll have a outa sight time.'

The woman on the floor cursed. Jimmie was intent upon his bruised forearms. The girl cast a glance about the room filled with a chaotic mass of débris, and at the writhing body of her mother.

'Git th' devil outa here.'

Maggie went.

CHAPTER 10

JIMMIE had an idea it wasn't common courtesy for a friend to come to one's home and ruin one's sister. But he was not sure how much Pete knew about the rules of politeness.

The following night he returned home from work at a rather late hour in the evening. In passing through the halls he came upon the gnarled and leathery old woman who possessed the music-box. She was grinning in the dim light that drifted through dust-stained panes. She beckoned to him with a smudged forefinger.

'Ah, Jimmie, what do yehs t'ink I tumbled to, las' night! It was deh funnies' t'ing I ever saw,' she cried, coming close to him and leering. She was trembling with eagerness to tell her tale. 'I was by me door las' night when yer sister and her jude feller came in late, oh, very late. An' she, the dear, she was a-cryin' as if her heart would break, she was. It was deh funnies' t'ing I ever saw. An' right out here by me door she asked him did he love her, did he. An' she was a-crying as if her heart would break, poor t'ing. An' him, I could see be deh way what he said it dat she had been askin' orften; he says, "Oh, gee, yes," he says, says he, "Oh, gee, yes."'

Storm clouds swept over Jimmie's face, but he turned from the leathery old woman and plodded on upstairs.

'Oh, gee, yes,' she called after him. She laughed a laugh that was like a prophetic croak.

There was no one in at home. The rooms showed that attempts had been made at tidying them. Parts of the wreckage of the day before had been repaired by an unskilled hand. A chair or two and the table stood uncertainly upon legs. The floor had been newly swept. The blue ribbons had been restored to the curtains, and the lambrequin, with its immense sheaves of yellow wheat and red roses of equal size, had been returned, in a worn and sorry state, to its place at the mantel. Maggie's jacket and hat were gone from the nail behind the door.

Jimmie walked to the window and began to look through the blurred glass. It occurred to him to wonder vaguely, for an instant, if some of the women of his acquaintance had brothers.

Suddenly, however, he began to swear.

'But he was me frien'! I brought 'im here! Dat's d' devil of it!'

He fumed about the room, his anger gradually rising to the furious pitch.

'I'll kill deh jay! Dat's what I'll do! I'll kill deh jay!'

He clutched his hat and sprang towards the door. But it opened and his mother's great form blocked the passage.

'What's d' matter wid yeh?' exclaimed she, coming into the rooms.

Jimmie gave vent to a sardonic curse and then laughed heavily.

'Well, Maggie's gone teh d' devil! Are yehs deaf?' roared Jimmie, impatiently.

'Aw, git out!' murmured the mother, astounded.

Jimmie grunted, and then began to stare out of the window. His mother sat down in a chair, but a moment later sprang erect and delivered a maddened whirl of oaths. Her son turned to look at her as she reeled and swayed in the middle of the room, her fierce face convulsed with passion, her blotched arms raised high in imprecation.

'May she be cursed for ever!' she shrieked. 'May she eat nothin' but stones and deh dirt in deh street. May she sleep in deh gutter an' never see deh sun shine again. D' bloomin'—'

42

'Here now,' said her son. 'Go fall on yerself, an' quit dat.'

The mother raised lamenting eyes to the ceiling.

'She's d' devil's own chil', Jimmie,' she whispered. 'Ah, who would tink such a bad girl could grow up in our fambly, Jimmie, me son. Many d' hour I've spent in talk wid dat girl an' tol' her if she ever went on d' streets I'd see her damned. An' after all her bringin' up an' what I tol' her and talked wid her, she goes teh d' bad, like a duck teh water.'

The tears rolled down her furrowed face. Her hands trembled.

'An' den when dat Sadie MacMallister next door to us was sent teh d' devil by dat feller what worked in d' soap factory, didn't I tell our Mag dat if she—'

'Ah, dat's anudder story,' interrupted the brother. 'Of course, dat Sadie was nice an' all dat—but—see—it ain't dessame as if—well, Maggie was diff'ent—see—she was diff'ent.'

He was trying to formulate a theory that he had always unconsciously held, that all sisters, excepting his own, could, advisedly, be ruined.

He suddenly broke out again. 'I'll go t'ump d' mug what done her d' harm. I'll kill 'im! He tinks he kin scrap, but when he gits me a-chasin' 'im he'll fin' out where he's wrong, d' big stuff! I'll wipe up d' street wid 'im.'

In a fury he plunged out of the doorway. As he vanished the mother raised her head and lifted both hands, entreating.

'May she be cursed for ever!' she cried.

In the darkness of the hallway Jimmie discerned a knot of women talking volubly. When he strode by they paid no attention to him.

'She allus was a bold thing,' he heard one of them cry in an eager voice. 'Dere wasn't a feller come teh deh house but she'd try teh mash 'im. My Annie says deh shameless t'ing tried teh ketch her feller, her own feller, what we useter know his fader.'

'I could a' tol' yehs dis two years ago,' said a woman, in a key of triumph. 'Yes, sir, it was over two years ago dat I says teh my ol' man, I says, "Dat Johnson girl ain't straight," I says. "Oh, rats!" he says. "Oh, hell!" "Dat's all right," I says, "but I know what I knows," I says, "an' it'll come out later. You wait an' see," I says, "you see."'

'Anybody what had eyes could see dat dere was somethin' wrong wid dat girl. I didn't like her actions.'

On the street Jimmie met a friend. 'What's wrong?' asked the latter.

Jimmie explained. 'An' I'll t'ump 'im till he can't stand.'

'Oh, go ahn!' said the friend. 'What's deh use! Yeh'll git pulled in! Everybody 'ill be onto it! An' ten plunks! Gee!'

Jimmie was determined. 'He t'inks he kin scrap, but he'll fin' out diff'ent.'

'Gee!' remonstrated the friend, 'what's d' use?'

CHAPTER 11

ON a corner a glass-fronted building shed a yellow glare upon the pavements. The open mouth of a saloon called seductively to passengers to enter and annihilate sorrow or create rage.

The interior of the place was prepared in olive and bronze tints of imitation leather. A shining bar of counterfeit massiveness extended down the side of the room. Behind it a great mahogany-imitation sideboard reached the ceiling. Upon its shelves rested pyramids of shimmering glasses that were never disturbed. Mirrors set in the face of the sideboard multiplied them. Lemons, oranges, and paper napkins, arranged with mathematical precision, sat among the glasses. Many-hued decanters of liquor perched at regular intervals on the lower shelves. A nickel-plated cash register occupied a place in the exact centre of the general effect. The elementary senses of it all seemed to be opulence and geometrical accuracy.

Across from the bar a smaller counter held a collection of plates upon which swarmed frayed fragments of crackers, slices of boiled ham, dishevelled bits of cheese, and pickles swimming in vinegar. An odour of grasping, begrimed hands and munching mouths pervaded all.

Pete, in a white jacket, was behind the bar bending expectantly towards a quiet stranger. 'A beeh,' said the man. Pete drew a foam-topped glassful, and set it dripping upon the bar.

At this moment the light bamboo doors at the entrance swung open and crashed against the wall. Jimmie and companion entered. They swaggered unsteadily belligerently towards the bar, and looked at Pete bleared and blinking eyes.

'Gin,' said Jimmie.

'Gin,' said the companion.

Pete slid a bottle and two glasses along the bar. He bent his head sideways as he assiduously polished away with a napkin at the gleaming wood. He wore a look of watchfulness.

Jimmie and his companion kept their eyes upon the bar-tender and conversed loudly in tones of contempt.

'He's a dandy masher, ain't he?' laughed Jimmie.

'Well, ain't he!' said the companion, sneering. 'He's great, he is. Git on to deh mug on deh blokie. Dat's enough to make a feller turn handsprings in 'is sleep.'

The quiet stranger moved himself and his glass a trifle farther away and maintained an attitude of obliviousness.

'Gee! ain't he hot stuff?'

'Git on to his shape!'

'Hey!' cried Jimmie, in tones of command. Pete came along slowly, with a sullen dropping of the under lip.

'Well,' he growled, 'what's eatin' yehs?'

'Gin,' said Jimmie.

'Gin,' said the companion.

As Pete confronted them with the bottle and the glasses they laughed in his face. Jimmie's companion, evidently overcome with merriment, pointed a grimy forefinger in Pete's direction.

'Say, Jimmie,' demanded he, 'what's dat behind d' bar?'

'Looks like some chump,' replied Jimmie. They laughed loudly. Pete put down a bottle with a bang and turned a formidable face towards them. He disclosed his teeth and his shoulders heaved restlessly.

'You fellers can't guy me,' he said. 'Drink yer stuff an' git out an' don' make no trouble.'

Instantly the laughter faded from the faces of the two men, and expressions of offended dignity immediately came.

46

'Aw, who has said any'ting t' you?' cried they in the same breath.

The quiet stranger looked at the door calculatingly.

'Ah, come off,' said Pete to the two men. 'Don' pick me up for no jay. Drink yer rum an' git out an' don' make no trouble.'

'Aw, go ahn!' airily cried Jimmie.

'Aw, go ahn!' airily repeated his companion.

'We goes when we git ready! See?' continued Jimmie.

'Well,' said Pete in a threatening voice, 'don' make no trouble.'

Jimmie suddenly leaned forward with his head on one side. He snarled like a wild animal.

'Well, what if we does? See?' said he.

Hot blood flushed into Pete's face, and he shot a lurid glance at Jimmie.

'Well, den we'll see who's d' bes' man, you or me,' he said.

The quiet stranger moved modestly towards the door.

Jimmie began to swell with valour.

'Don' pick me up fer no tenderfoot. When yeh tackles me yeh tackles one of d' bes' men in d' city. See? I'm a scrapper, I am. Ain't dat right, Billie?'

'Sure, Mike,' responded his companion in tones of conviction.

'Aw!' said Pete, easily. 'Go fall on yerself.'

The two men again began to laugh.

'What is dat talking?' cried the companion.

'Don' ast me,' replied Jimmie with exaggerated contempt.

Pete made a furious gesture. 'Git outa here now, an' don' make no trouble. See? Youse fellers er lookin' fer a scrap, an' it's like yeh'll fin' one if yeh keeps on shootin' off yer mout's. I knows yehs! See? I kin lick better men dan yehs ever saw in yer lifes. Dat's right! See? Don' pick me up fer no stuff, er yeh might be jolted out in d' street

47

before yeh knows where yeh is. When I comes from behind dis bar, I t'rows yehs boat inteh d' street. See?'

'Ah, go ahn!' cried the two men in chorus.

The glare of a panther came into Pete's eyes. 'Dat's what I said! Unnerstan'?'

He came through a passage at the end of the bar and swelled down upon the two men. They stepped promptly forward and crowded close to him.

They bristled like three roosters. They moved their heads pugnaciously and kept their shoulders braced. The nervous muscles about each mouth twitched with a forced smile of mockery.

'Well, what yer goin' t' do?' gritted Jimmie.

Pete stepped warily back, waving his hands before him to keep the men from coming too near.

'Well, what yer goin' t' do?' repeated Jimmie's ally. They kept close to him, taunting and leering. They strove to make him attempt the initial blow.

'Keep back now! Don' crowd me,' said Pete ominously.

Again they chorused in contempt. 'Aw, go ahn!'

In a small, tossing group, the three men edged for positions like frigates contemplating battle.

'Well, why don' yeh try t' t'row us out?' cried Jimmie and his ally with copious sneers.

The bravery of bulldogs sat upon the faces of the men. Their clinched fists moved like eager weapons.

The allied two jostled the bar-tender's elbows, glaring at him with feverish eyes and forcing him toward the wall.

Suddenly Pete swore furiously. The flash of action gleamed from his eyes. He threw back his arm and aimed a tremendous, lightning-like blow at Jimmie's face. His foot swung a step forward and the weight of his body was behind his fist. Jimmie ducked his head, Bowery-like, with the quickness of a cat. The fierce, answering blows of Jimmie and his ally crushed on Pete's bowed head.

The quiet stranger vanished.

The arms of the combatants whirled in the air like flails. The faces of the men, at first flushed to flame-coloured anger, now began to fade to the pallor of warriors in the blood and heat of a battle. Their lips curled back and stretched tightly over the gums in ghoul-like grins. Through their white, gripped teeth struggled hoarse whisperings of oaths. Their eyes glittered with murderous fire.

Each head was huddled between its owner's shoulders, and arms were swinging with marvellous rapidity. Feet scraped to and fro with a loud scratching sound upon the sanded floors. Blows left crimson blotches upon the pale skin. The curses of the first quarter-minute of the fight died away. The breaths of the fighters came wheezing from their lips and the three chests were straining and heaving. Pete at intervals gave vent to low, laboured hisses, that sounded like a desire to kill. Jimmie's ally gibbered at times like a wounded maniac. Jimmie was silent, fighting with the face of a sacrificial priest. The rage of fear shone in all their eyes and their blood-coloured fists whirled.

At a critical moment a blow from Pete's hand struck the ally and he crashed to the floor. He wriggled instantly to his feet, and grasping the quiet stranger's beer glass from the bar, hurled it at Pete's head.

High on the wall it burst like a bomb, shivering fragments flying in all directions. Then missiles came to every man's hand. The place had heretofore appeared free of things to throw, but suddenly glasses and bottles went singing through the air. They were thrown point-blank at bobbing heads. The pyramids of shimmering glasses, that had never been disturbed, changed to cascades as heavy bottles were flung into them. Mirrors splintered to nothing.

The three frothing creatures on the floor buried themselves in a frenzy for blood. There followed in the wake of missiles and fists some unknown prayers, perhaps for death.

The quiet stranger had sprawled very pyrotechnically out on the sidewalk. A laugh ran up and down the avenue for the half of a block.

'Dey've t'rowed a bloke inteh deh street.'

People heard the sound of breaking glass and shuffling feet within the saloon and came running. A small group, bending down to look under the bamboo doors, and watching the fall of glass and three pairs of violent legs, changed in a moment to a crowd.

A policeman came charging down the sidewalk and bounced through the doors into the saloon. The crowd bent and surged in absorbing anxiety to see.

Jimmie caught the first sight of the oncoming interruption. On his feet he had the same regard for a policeman that, when on his truck, he had for a fire-engine. He howled and ran for the side door.

The officer made a terrific advance, club in hand. One comprehensive sweep of the long night stick threw the ally to the floor and forced Pete to a corner. With his disengaged hand he made a furious effort at Jimmie's coat-tails. Then he regained his balance and paused.

'Well, well, you are a pair of pictures. What have ye been up to?'

Jimmie, with his face drenched in blood, escaped up a side street, pursued a short distance by some of the more law-loving or excited individuals of the crowd.

Later, from a safe dark corner, he saw the policeman, the ally, and the bar-tender emerge from the saloon. Pete locked the doors and then followed up the avenue in the rear of the crowd-encompassed policeman and his charge.

At first Jimmie, with his heart throbbing at battle heat, started to go desperately to the rescue of his friend, but he halted.

'Ah, what's d' use?' he demanded of himself.

CHAPTER 12

In a hall of irregular shape sat Pete and Maggie drinking beer. A submissive orchestra, dictated to by a spectacled man with frowsy hair and in soiled evening dress, industriously followed the bobs of his head and the waves of his baton. A ballad singer, in a gown of flaming scarlet sang in the inevitable voice of brass. When she vanished, men seated at the tables near the front applauded loudly, pounding the polished wood with their beer glasses. She returned attired in less gown, and sang again. She received another enthusiastic encore. She reappeared in still less gown and danced. The deafening rumble of glasses and clapping of hands that followed her exit indicated an overwhelming desire to have her come on for the fourth time, but the curiosity of the audience was not gratified.

Maggie was pale. From her eyes had been plucked all look of self-reliance. She leaned with a depending air towards her companion. She was timid, as if fearing his anger or displeasure. She seemed to beseech tenderness of him.

Pete's air of distinguished valour had grown upon him until it threatened to reach stupendous dimensions. He was infinitely gracious to the girl. It was apparent to her that his condescension was a marvel.

He could appear to strut even while sitting still, and he showed that he was a lion of lordly characteristics by the air with which he spat.

With Maggie gazing at him wonderingly, he took pride in commanding the waiters, who were, however, indifferent, or deaf.

'Hi, you, git a russle on yehs! What yehs lookin' at? Two more beehs, d' yeh hear?'

He leaned back and critically regarded the person of a girl with a straw-coloured wig who was flinging her heels about up on the stage in somewhat awkward imitation of a well-known *danseuse*.

At times Maggie told Pete long confidential tales of her former home life, dwelling upon the escapades of the other members of the family and the difficulties she had had to combat in order to obtain a degree of comfort. He responded in the accents of philanthropy. He pressed her arm with an air of reassuring proprietorship.

'Dey was cursed jays,' he said, denouncing the mother and brother.

The sound of the music which, through the efforts of the frowsy-headed leader, drifted to her ears in the smoke-filled atmosphere, made the girl dream. She thought of her former Rum Alley environment and turned to regard Pete's strong protecting fists. She thought of a collar-and-cuff manufactory and the eternal moan of the proprietor: 'What een hale do you sink I pie fife dolla a week for? Play? No, py tamn!' She contemplated Pete's man-subduing eyes and noted that wealth and prosperity were indicated by his clothes. She imagined a future, rose-tinted, because of its distance from all that she had experienced before.

As to the present she perceived only vague reasons to be miserable. Her life was Pete's, and she considered him worthy of the charge. She would be disturbed by no particular apprehensions so long as Pete adored her as he now said he did. She did not feel like a bad woman. To her knowledge she had never seen any better.

At times men at other tables regarded the girl furtively. Pete, aware of it, nodded to her and grinned. He felt proud.

'Mag, yer a bloomin' good-looker,' he remarked, studying her face through the haze. The men made

Maggie fear, but she blushed at Pete's words as it became apparent to her that she was the apple of his eye.

Grey-headed men, wonderfully pathetic in their dissipation, stared at her through clouds. Smooth-cheeked boys, some of them with faces of stone and mouths of sin, not nearly so pathetic as the grey heads, tried to find the girl's eyes in the smoke wreaths. Maggie considered she was not what they thought her. She confined her glances to Pete and the stage.

The orchestra played Negro melodies, and a versatile drummer pounded, whacked, clattered, and scratched on a dozen machines to make noise.

Those glances of the men shot at Maggie from under half-closed lids made her tremble. She thought them all to be worse men than Pete.

'Come, let's go,' she said.

As they went out Maggie perceived two women seated at a table with some men. They were painted, and their cheeks had lost their roundness. As she passed them the girl, with a shrinking movement, drew back her skirts.

CHAPTER 13

JIMMIE did not return home for a number of days after the fight with Pete in the saloon. When he did, he approached with extreme caution.

He found his mother raving. Maggie had not returned home. The parent continually wondered how her daughter could come to such a pass. She had never considered Maggie as a pearl dropped unstained into Rum Alley from Heaven, but she could not conceive how it was possible for her daughter to fall so low as to bring disgrace upon her family. She was terrific in denunciation of the girl's wickedness.

The fact that the neighbours talked of it maddened her. When women came in, and in the course of their conversation casually asked, 'Where's Maggie these days?' the mother shook her fuzzy head at them and appalled them with curses. Cunning hints inviting confidence she rebuffed with violence.

'An' wid all d' bringin'-up she had, how could she?' moaningly she asked of her son. 'Wid all d' talkin' wid her I did an' d' t'ings I tol' her to remember. When a girl is bringed up d' way I bringed up Maggie, how kin she go teh d' devil?'

Jimmie was transfixed by these questions. He could not conceive how, under the circumstances, his mother's daughter and his sister could have been so wicked.

His mother took a drink from a bottle that sat on the table. She continued her lament.

'She had a bad heart dat girl did, Jimmie. She was wicked t' d' heart an' we never knowed it.'

Jimmie nodded, admitting the fact.

'We lived in d' same house wid her an' I brought her up, an' we never knowed how bad she was.'

Jimmie nodded again.

'Wid a home like dis an' a mudder like me, she went teh d' bad,' cried the mother, raising her eyes.

One day Jimmie came home, sat down in a chair, and began to wriggle about with a new and strange nervousness. At last he spoke shamefacedly.

'Well, look-a-here, dis t'ing queers us! See? W'ere queered! An' maybe it 'ud be better if I—well, I t'ink I kin look 'er up an'—maybe it 'ud be better if I fetched her home an'—'

The mother started from the chair and broke forth into a storm of passionate anger.

'What! Let 'er come an' sleep under deh same roof wid her mudder agin! Oh, yes, I will, won't I! Sure? Shame on yehs, Jimmie Johnson, fer sayin' such a t'ing teh yer own mudder! Little did I t'ink when yehs was a babby playin' about me feet dat ye'd grow up teh say such a t'ing teh yer mudder—yer own mudder. I never taut—'

Sobs choked her and interrupted her reproaches.

'Dere ain't nottin' teh make sech trouble about,' said Jimmie. 'I on'y says it 'ud be better if we keep dis t'ing dark, see? It queers us! See?'

His mother laughed a laugh that seemed to ring through the city and be echoed and re-echoed by countless other laughs. 'Oh, yes, I will, won't I! Sure!'

'Well, yeh must take me fer a damn fool,' said Jimmie, indignant at his mother for mocking him. 'I didn't say we'd make 'er inteh a little tin angel, ner nottin', but deh way it is now she can queer us! Don'che see?'

'Aye, she'll git tired of deh life atter a while an' den she'll wanna be a-comin' home, won' she, deh beast! I'll let 'er in den, won' I?'

'Well, I didn't mean none of dis prod'gal bus'ness anyway,' explained Jimmie.

'It wa'n't no prod'gal dauter, yeh fool,' said the mother. 'It was prod'gal son, anyhow.'

'I know dat,' said Jimmie.

For a time they sat in silence. The mother's eyes gloated on the scene which her imagination called before her. Her lips were set in a vindictive smile.

'Aye, she'll cry, won' she, an' carry on, an' tell how Pete, or some odder feller, beats 'er, an' she'll say she's sorry an' all dat, an' she ain't happy, she ain't, and she wants to come home again, she does.'

With grim humour the mother imitated the possible wailing notes of the daughter's voice.

'Den I'll take 'er in, won't I? She kin cry 'er two eyes out on deh stones of deh street before I'll dirty d' place wid her. She abused an' ill-treated her own mudder— her own mudder what loved her, and she'll never git anodder chance.'

Jimmie thought he had a great idea of women's frailty, but he could not understand why any of his kind should be victims.

'Curse her!' he said fervidly.

Again he wondered vaguely if some of the women of his acquaintance had brothers. Nevertheless, his mind did not for an instant confuse himself with those brothers nor his sister with theirs. After the mother had, with great difficulty, suppressed the neighbours, she went among them and proclaimed her grief. 'May Heaven forgive dat girl,' was her continual cry. To attentive ears she recited the whole length and breadth of her woes.

'I bringed 'er up deh way a dauter oughta be bringed up, an' dis is how she served me! She went teh deh devil deh first chance she got! May Heaven forgive her.'

When arrested for drunkenness she used the story of her daughter's downfall with telling effect upon the police justices. Finally one of them said to her, peering down over his spectacles: 'Mary, the records of this and other courts show that you are the mother of forty-two daughters who have been ruined. The case is unparalleled in the annals of this court, and this court thinks—'

The mother went through life shedding large tears of sorrow. Her red face was a picture of agony.

Of course Jimmie publicly damned his sister that he might appear on a higher social plane. But, arguing with himself, stumbling about in ways that he knew not, he, once, almost came to a conclusion that his sister would have been more firmly good had she better known why. However, he felt that he could not hold such a view. He threw it hastily aside.

CHAPTER 14

In a hilarious hall there were twenty-eight tables and twenty-eight women and a crowd of smoking men. Valiant noise was made on a stage at the end of the hall by an orchestra composed of men who looked as if they had just happened in. Soiled waiters ran to and fro, swooping down like hawks on the unwary in the throng; clattering along the aisles with trays covered with glasses; stumbling over women's skirts and charging two prices for everything but beer, all with a swiftness that blurred the view of the cocoanut palms and dusty monstrosities painted upon the walls of the room. A 'bouncer', with an immense load of business upon his hands, plunged about in the crowd, dragging bashful strangers to prominent chairs, ordering waiters here and there, and quarrelling furiously with men who wanted to sing with the orchestra.

The usual smoke cloud was present, but so dense that heads and arms seemed entangled in it. The rumble of conversation was replaced by a roar. Plenteous oaths heaved through the air. The room rang with the shrill voices of women bubbling over with drink laughter. The chief element in the music of the orchestra was speed. The musicians played in intent fury. A woman was singing and smiling upon the stage, but no one took notice of her. The rate at which the piano, cornet, and violins were going, seemed to impart wildness to the half-drunken crowd. Beer glasses were emptied at a gulp and conversation became a rapid chatter. The smoke eddied and swirled like a shadowy river hurrying towards some unseen falls. Pete and Maggie entered the hall and took chairs at a table near the door. The woman who was seated there made an attempt to occupy Pete's attention, and, failing, went away.

Three weeks had passed since the girl had left home. The air of spaniel-like dependence had been magnified and showed its direct effect in the peculiar off-handedness and ease of Pete's way towards her.

She followed Pete's eyes with hers, anticipating with smiles gracious looks from him.

A woman of brilliance and audacity, accompanied by a mere boy, came into the place and took a seat near them.

At once Pete sprang to his feet, his face beaming with glad surprise.

'Hully gee, dere's Nellie!' he cried.

He went over to the table and held out an eager hand to the woman.

'Why, hello, Pete, me boy, how are you?' said she, giving him her fingers.

Maggie took instant note of the woman. She perceived that her black dress fitted her to perfection. Her linen collar and cuffs were spotless. Tan gloves were stretched over her well-shaped hands. A hat of a prevailing fashion perched jauntily upon her dark hair. She wore no jewelry and was painted with no apparent paint. She looked clear-eyed through the stares of the men.

'Sit down, and call your lady friend over,' she said to Pete. At his beckoning Maggie came and sat between Pete and the mere boy.

'I thought yeh were gone away fer good,' began Pete, at once. 'When did yeh git back? How did dat Buff'lo bus'-ness turn out?'

The woman shrugged her shoulders. 'Well, he didn't have as many stamps as he tried to make out, so I shook him, that's all.'

'Well, I'm glad teh see yehs back in deh city,' said Pete, with gallantry.

He and the woman entered into a long conversation,

exchanging reminiscences of days together. Maggie sat still, unable to formulate an intelligent sentence as her addition to the conversation and painfully aware of it.

She saw Pete's eyes sparkle as he gazed upon the handsome stranger. He listened smilingly to all she said. The woman was familiar with all his affairs, asked him about mutual friends, and knew the amount of his salary.

She paid no attention to Maggie, looking towards her once or twice and apparently seeing the wall beyond.

The mere boy was sulky. In the beginning he had welcomed the additions with acclamations.

'Let's all have a drink! What'll you take, Nell? And you, Miss What's-your-name. Have a drink, Mr——you, I mean.

He had shown a sprightly desire to do the talking for the company and tell all about his family. In a loud voice he declaimed on various topics. He assumed a patronizing air towards Pete. As Maggie was silent, he paid no attention to her. He made a great show of lavishing wealth upon the woman of brilliance and audacity.

'Do keep still, Freddie! You talk like a clock,' said the woman to him. She turned away and devoted her attention to Pete.

'We'll have many a good time together again, eh?'

'Sure, Nell,' said Pete, enthusiastic at once.

'Say,' whispered she, leaning forward, 'let's go over to Billie's and have a time.'

'Well, it's dis way! See?' said Pete. 'I got dis lady frien' here.'

'Oh, g'way with her,' argued the woman. Pete appeared disturbed.

'All right,' said she, nodding her head at him. 'All right for you! We'll see the next time you ask me to go anywheres with you.'

Pete squirmed.

'Say,' he said, beseechingly, 'come wid me a minit an'
I'll tel yer why.'

The woman waved her hand.

'Oh, that's all right, you needn't explain, you know.
You wouldn't come merely because you wouldn't come,
that's all.'

To Pete's visible distress she turned to the mere boy,
bringing him speedily out of a terrific rage. He had been
debating whether it would be the part of a man to pick a
quarrel with Pete, or would he be justified in striking him
savagely with his beer glass without warning. But he re-
covered himself when the woman turned to renew her
smilings. He beamed upon her with an expression that
was somewhat tipsy and inexpressibly tender.

'Say, shake that Bowery jay,' requested he, in a loud
whisper.

'Freddie, you are so funny,' she replied.

Pete reached forward and touched the woman on the
arm.

'Come out a minit while I tells yeh why I can't go wid
yer. Yer doin' me dirt, Nell! I never taut ye'd do me dirt,
Nell. Come on, will yer?' He spoke in tones of injury.

'Why, I don't see why I should be interested in your
explanations,' said the woman, with a coldness that
seemed to reduce Pete to a pulp.

His eyes pleaded with her. 'Come out a minit while I
tells yeh. On d' level, now.'

The woman nodded slightly at Maggie and the mere
boy, saying, ' 'Scuse me.'

The mere boy interrupted his loving smile and turned
a shrivelling glare upon Pete. His boyish countenance
flushed and he spoke in a whine to the woman:

'Oh, I say, Nellie, this ain't a square deal, you know.
You aren't goin' to leave me and go off with that duffer,
are you? I should think—'

'Why, you dear boy, of course I'm not,' cried the

woman, affectionately. She bent over and whispered in his ear. He smiled again and settled in his chair as if resolved to wait patiently.

As the woman walked down between the rows of tables, Pete was at her shoulder talking earnestly, apparently in explanation. The woman waved her hands with studied airs of indifference. The doors swung behind them, leaving Maggie and the mere boy seated at the table.

Maggie was dazed. She could dimly perceive that something stupendous had happened. She wondered why Pete saw fit to remonstrate with the woman, pleading forgiveness with his eyes. She thought she noted an air of submission about her leonine Pete. She was astounded.

The mere boy occupied himself with cocktails and a cigar. He was tranquilly silent for half an hour. Then he bestirred himself and spoke.

'Well,' he said, sighing, 'I knew this was the way it would be. They got cold feet.' There was another stillness. The mere boy seemed to be musing.

'She was pulling m' leg. That's the whole amount of it,' he said suddenly. 'It's a bloomin' shame the way that girl does. Why, I've spent over two dollars in drinks tonight. And she goes off with that plug-ugly, who looks as if he had been hit in the face with a coin die. I call it rocky treatment for a fellah like me. Here, waiter, bring me a cocktail, and make it strong.'

Maggie made no reply. She was watching the doors. 'It's a mean piece of business,' complained the mere boy. He explained to her how amazing it was that anybody should treat him in such a manner. 'But I'll get square with her, you bet. She won't get far ahead of yours truly, you know,' he added, winking. 'I'll tell her plainly that it was bloomin' mean business. And she won't come it over me with any of her "now-Freddie-dears." She thinks my name is Freddie, you know, but of course it ain't. I always tell these people some name like that, because if they got on to your right name they might use it some time. Understand? Oh, they don't fool me much.'

Maggie was paying no attention, being intent upon the doors. The mere boy relapsed into a period of gloom, during which he exterminated a number of cocktails with a determined air, as if replying defiantly to fate. He occasionally broke forth into sentences composed of invectives joined together in a long chain.

The girl was still staring at the doors. After a time the mere boy began to see cobwebs just in front of his nose. He spurred himself into being agreeable and insisted upon her having a charlotte russe and a glass of beer.

'They's gone,' he remarked, 'they's gone.' He looked at her through the smoke wreaths. 'Shay, lil' girl, we mightish well make bes' of it. You ain't such bad-lookin' girl, y'know. Not half bad. Can't come up to Nell, though. No, can't do it! Well, I should shay not! Nell fine-lookin' girl! F—i—n—ine. You look bad longsider her, but by y'self ain't so bad. Have to do anyhow. Nell gone. O'ny you left. Not half bad though.'

Maggie stood up.

'I'm going home,' she said.

The mere boy started.

'Eh? What? Home,' he cried, struck with amazement. 'I beg pardon, did hear say home?'

'I'm going home,' she repeated.

'Great heavens! what hav'a struck?' demanded the mere boy of himself, stupefied.

In a semi-comatose state he conducted her on board an uptown car, ostentatiously paid her fare, leered kindly at her through the rear window, and fell off the steps.

CHAPTER 15

A FORLORN woman went along a lighted avenue. The street was filled with people desperately bound on missions. An endless crowd darted at the elevated station stairs, and the horse cars were thronged with owners of bundles.

The pace of the forlorn woman was slow. She was apparently searching for some one. She loitered near the doors of saloons and watched men emerge from them. She furtively scanned the faces in the rushing stream of pedestrians. Hurrying men, bent on catching some boat or train, jostled her elbows, failing to notice her, their thoughts fixed on distant dinners.

The forlorn woman had a peculiar face. Her smile was no smile. But when in repose her features had a shadowy look that was like a sardonic grin, as if some one had sketched with cruel forefinger indelible lines about her mouth.

Jimmie came strolling up the avenue. The woman encountered him with an aggrieved air.

'Oh, Jimmie, I've been lookin' all over for yehs—' she began.

Jimmie made an important gesture and quickened his pace.

'Ah, don't bodder me!' he said, with the savageness of a man whose life is pestered.

The woman followed him along the sidewalk in somewhat the manner of a suppliant.

'But, Jimmie,' she said, 'yehs told me yehs—'

Jimmie turned upon her fiercely, as if resolved to make a last stand for comfort and peace.

'Say, Hattie, don' foller me from one end of deh city

teh de odder. Let up, will yehs! Give me a minute's res', can't yehs? Yehs makes me tired, allus taggin' me. See? Ain't yehs got no sense? Do yehs want people teh get on to me? Go chase yourself.'

The woman stepped closer and laid her fingers on his arm. 'But, look-a-here—'

Jimmie snarled. 'Oh, go teh blazes!'

He darted into the front door of a convenient saloon and a moment later came out into the shadows that surrounded the side door. On the brilliantly lighted avenue he perceived the forlorn woman dodging about like a scout. Jimmie laughed with an air of relief and went away.

When he arrived home he found his mother clamouring. Maggie had returned. She stood shivering beneath the torrent of her mother's wrath.

'Well, I'm damned!' said Jimmie in greeting.

His mother, tottering about the room, pointed a quivering forefinger.

'Look ut her, Jimmie, look ut her. Dere's yer sister, boy. Dere's yer sister. Look ut her! Look ut her!'

She screamed at Maggie with scoffing laughter.

The girl stood in the middle of the room. She edged about as if unable to find a place on the floor to put her feet.

'Ha, ha, ha!' bellowed the mother. 'Dere she stands! Ain't she purty? Look ut her! Ain' she sweet, deh beast? Look ut her! Ha, ha! look ut her!'

She lurched forward and put her red and seamed hands upon her daughter's face. She bent down and peered keenly up into the eyes of the girl.

'Oh, she's jes' dessame as she ever was, ain' she? She's her mudder's putty darlin' yit, ain' she? Look ut her, Jimmie. Come here and look ut her.'

The loud, tremendous railing of the mother brough the denizens of the Rum Alley tenement to their doors.

65

Women came in the hallways. Children scurried to and fro.

'What's up? Dat Johnson party on anudder tear?'

'Naw! Young Mag's come home!'

'Git out!'

Through the open doors curious eyes stared in at Maggie. Children ventured into the room and ogled her as if they formed the front row at a theatre. Women, without, bent towards each other and whispered, nodding their heads with airs of profound philosophy.

A baby, overcome with curiosity concerning this object at which all were looking, sidled forward and touched her dress, cautiously, as if investigating a red-hot stove. Its mother's voice rang out like a warning trumpet. She rushed forward and grabbed her child, casting a terrible look of indignation at the girl.

Maggie's mother paced to and fro, addressing the doorful of eyes, expounding like a glib showman. Her voice rang through the building.

'Dere she stands,' she cried, wheeling suddenly and pointing with dramatic finger. 'Dere she stands! Look ut her! Ain' she a dindy? An' she was so good as to come home teh her mudder, she was! Ain' she a beaut'? Ain' she a dindy?'

The jeering cries ended in another burst of shrill laughter.

The girl seemed to awaken. 'Jimmie—'

He drew hastily back from her.

'Well, now, yer a t'ing, ain' yeh?' he said, his lips curling in scorn. Radiant virtue sat upon his brow and his repelling hands expressed horror of contamination.

Maggie turned and went.

The crowd at the door fell back precipitately.

A baby falling down in front of the door wrenched a scream like that of a wounded animal from its mother. Another woman sprang forward and picked it up with a chivalrous air, as if rescuing a human being from an on-coming express train.

As the girl passed down through the hall, she went before open doors framing more eyes strangely micro-scopic, and sending broad beams of inquisitive light into the darkness of her path. On the second floor she met the gnarled old woman who possessed the music-box.

'So,' she cried, ' 'ere yehs are back again, are yehs? An' dey've kicked yehs out? Well, come in an' stay wid me t'night. I ain' got no moral standin'.'

From above came an unceasing babble of tongues, over all of which rang the mother's derisive laughter.

CHAPTER 16

PETE did not consider that he had ruined Maggie. If he had thought that her soul could never smile again, he would have believed the mother and brother, who were pyrotechnic over the affair, to be responsible for it.

Besides, in his world, souls did not insist upon being able to smile. 'What d' hell?'

He felt a trifle entangled. It distressed him. Revelations and scenes might bring him the wrath of the owner of the saloon, who insisted upon respectability of an advanced type.

'What do dey wanna' raise such a smoke about it fer?' demanded he of himself, disgusted with the attitude of the family. He saw no necessity that people should lose their equilibrium merely because their sister or their daughter had stayed away from home.

Searching about in his mind for possible reasons for their conduct, he came upon the conclusion that Maggie's motives were correct, but that the two others wished to snare him. He felt pursued.

The woman whom he had met in the hilarious hall showed a disposition to ridicule him.

'A little pale thing with no spirit,' she said. 'Did you note the expression of her eyes? There was something in them about pumpkin-pie and virtue. That is a peculiar way the left corner of her mouth has of twitching, isn't it? Dear, dear, Pete, what are you coming to?'

Pete asserted at once that he never was very much interested in the girl. The woman interrupted him, laughing.

'Oh, it's not of the slightest consequence to me, my dear young man. You needn't draw maps for my benefit. Why should I be concerned about it?'

But Pete continued with his explanations. If he was laughed at for his tastes in women, he felt obliged to say that they were only temporary or indifferent ones.

The morning after Maggie had departed from home Pete stood behind the bar. He was immaculate in white jacket and apron and his hair was plastered over his brow with infinite correctness. No customers were in the place. Pete was twisting his napkined fist slowly in a beer glass, softly whistling to himself, and occasionally holding the object of his attention between his eyes and a few weak beams of sunlight that found their way over the thick screens and into the shaded rooms.

With lingering thoughts of the woman of brilliance and audacity, the bar-tender raised his head and stared through the varying cracks between the swaying bamboo doors. Suddenly the whistling pucker faded from his lips. He saw Maggie walking slowly past. He gave a great start, fearing for the previously mentioned eminent respectability of the place.

He threw a swift, nervous glance about him, all at once feeling guilty. No one was in the room.

He went hastily over to the side door. Opening it and looking out, he perceived Maggie standing, as if undecided, at the corner. She was searching the place with her eyes.

As she turned her face towards him, Pete beckoned to her hurriedly, intent upon returning with speed to a position behind the bar, and to the atmosphere of respectability upon which the proprietor insisted.

Maggie came to him, the anxious look disappearing from her face and a smile wreathing her lips.

'Oh, Pete—' she began brightly.

The bar-tender made a violent gesture of impatience.

'Oh, say,' cried he vehemently. 'What d' yeh wanna hang aroun' here fer? Do yer wanna git me inteh trouble?' he demanded with an air of injury.

Astonishment swept over the girl's features. 'Why, Pete! yehs tol' me—'

Pete's glance expressed profound irritation. His countenance reddened with the anger of a man whose respectability is being threatened.

'Say, yehs makes me tired! See? What d' yeh wanna tag aroun' atter me fer? Yeh'll do me dirt wid d' ol' man an' dey'll be trouble! If he sees a woman roun' here he'll go crazy an' I'll lose me job! See? Ain' yehs got no sense? Don' be allus bodderin' me. See? Yer brudder came in here an' made trouble an' d' ol' man hada put up fer it! An' now I'm done! See? I'm done.'

The girl's eyes stared into his face. 'Pete, don' yeh remem—'

'Oh, go ahn!' interrupted Pete, anticipating.

The girl seemed to have a struggle with herself. She was apparently bewildered and could not find speech. Finally she asked in a low voice, 'But where kin I go?'

The question exasperated Pete beyond the powers of endurance. It was a direct attempt to give him some responsibility in a matter that did not concern him. In his indignation he volunteered information.

'Oh, go to hell!' cried he. He slammed the door furiously and returned, with an air of relief, to his respectability.

Maggie went away.

She wandered aimlessly for several blocks. She stopped once and asked aloud a question of herself: 'Who?'

A man who was passing near her shoulder humorously took the questioning word as intended for him.

'Eh? What? Who? Nobody! I didn't say anything,' he laughingly said, and continued his way.

Soon the girl discovered that if she walked with such apparent aimlessness, some men looked at her with calculating eyes. She quickened her steps, frightened. As a protection, she adopted a demeanour of intentness as if going somewhere.

After a time she left rattling avenues and passed between rows of houses with sternness and stolidity stamped upon their features. She hung her head, for she felt their eyes grimly upon her.

Suddenly she came upon a stout gentleman in a silk hat and a chaste black coat, whose decorous row of buttons reached from his chin to his knees. The girl had heard of the grace of God and she decided to approach this man.

His beaming, chubby face was a picture of benevolence and kind-heartedness. His eyes shone goodwill.

But as the girl timidly accosted him, he made a convulsive movement and saved his respectability by a vigorous side step. He did not risk it to save a soul. For how was he to know that there was a soul before him that needed saving?

CHAPTER 17

Upon a wet evening, several months after the last chapter, two interminable rows of cars, pulled by slipping horses, jangled along a prominent side street. A dozen cabs, with coat-enshrouded drivers, clattered to and fro. Electric lights, whirring softly, shed a blurred radiance. A flower-dealer, his feet tapping impatiently, his nose and his wares glistening with raindrops, stood behind an array of roses and chrysanthemums. Two or three theatres emptied a crowd upon the storm-swept pavements. Men pulled their hats over their eyebrows and raised their collars to their ears. Women shrugged impatient shoulders in their warm cloaks and stopped to arrange their skirts for a walk through the storm. People who had been constrained to comparative silence for two hours burst into a roar of conversation, their hearts still kindling from the glowings of the stage.

The pavements became tossing seas of umbrellas. Men stepped forth to hail cabs or cars, raising their fingers in varied forms of polite request or imperative demand. An endless procession wended towards elevated stations. An atmosphere of pleasure and prosperity seemed to hang over the throng, born, perhaps, of good clothes and of two hours in a place of forgetfulness.

In the mingled light and gloom of an adjacent park, a handful of wet wanderers, in attitudes of chronic dejection, were scattered among the benches.

A girl of the painted cohorts of the city went along the street. She threw changing glances at men who passed her, giving smiling invitations to those of rural or untaught pattern and usually seeming sedately unconscious of the men with a metropolitan seal upon their faces.

Crossing glittering avenues, she went into the throng

emerging from the places of forgetfulness. She hurried forward through the crowd as if intent upon reaching a distant home, bending forward in her handsome cloak, daintily lifting her skirts, and picking for her well-shod feet the dryer spots upon the pavements.

The restless doors of saloons, clashing to and fro, disclosed animated rows of men before bars and hurrying bar-keepers.

A concert-hall gave to the street faint sounds of swift, machine-like music, as if a group of phantom musicians were hastening.

A tall young man, smoking a cigarette with a sublime air, strolled near the girl. He had on evening dress, a moustache, a chrysanthemum, and a look of ennui, all of which he kept carefully under his eye. Seeing the girl walk on as if such a young man as he was not in existence, he looked back transfixed with interest. He stared glassily for a moment, but gave a slight convulsive start when he discerned that she was neither new, Parisian, nor theatrical. He wheeled about hastily and turned his stare into the air, like a sailor with a searchlight.

A stout gentleman, with pompous and philanthropic whiskers, went stolidly by, the broad of his back sneering at the girl.

A belated man in business clothes, and in haste to catch a car, bounced against her shoulder. 'Hi, there, Mary, I beg your pardon! Brace up, old girl.' He grasped her arm to steady her, and then was away running down the middle of the street.

The girl walked on out of the realm of restaurants and saloons. She passed more glittering avenues and went into darker blocks than those where the crowd travelled.

A young man in light overcoat and Derby hat received a glance shot keenly from the eyes of the girl. He stopped and looked at her, thrusting his hands in his pockets and making a mocking smile curl his lips. 'Come, now, old lady,' he said, 'you don't mean to tell me that you sized me up for a farmer?'

A labouring man marched along with bundles under his arms. To her remarks, he replied, 'It's a fine evenin', ain't it?'

She smiled squarely into the face of a boy who was hurrying by with his hands buried in his overcoat pocket, his blond locks bobbing on his youthful temples, and a cheery smile of unconcern upon his lips. He turned his head and smiled back at her, waving his hands.

'Not this eve—some other eve.'

A drunken man, reeling in her pathway, began to roar at her. 'I ain' ga no money!' he shouted, in a dismal voice. He lurched on up the street, wailing to himself: 'I ain' ga no money. Ba' luck. Ain' ga no more money.'

The girl went into the gloomy districts near the river, where the tall black factories shut in the street and only occasional broad beams of light fell across the pavements from saloons. In front of one of these places, whence came the sound of a violin vigorously scraped, the patter of feet on boards and the ring of loud laughter, there stood a man with blotched features.

Further on in the darkness she met a ragged being with shifting, bloodshot eyes and grimy hands.

She went into the blackness of the final block. The shutters of the tall buildings were closed like grim lips. The structures seemed to have eyes that looked over them, beyond them, at other things. Afar off the lights of the avenues glittered as if from an impossible distance. Street-car bells jingled with a sound of merriment.

At the feet of the tall buildings appeared the deathly black hue of the river. Some hidden factory sent up a yellow glare, that lit for a moment the waters lapping oilily against timbers. The varied sounds of life, made joyous by distance and seeming unapproachableness, came faintly and died away to a silence.

74

In a partitioned-off section of a saloon sat a man with a half-dozen women, gleefully laughing, hovering about him. The man had arrived at that stage of drunkenness where affection is felt for the universe.

'I'm good f'ler, girls,' he said, convincingly. 'I'm good f'ler. An'body treats me right, I allus trea's zem right! See?'

The women nodded their heads approvingly. 'To be sure,' they cried in hearty chorus. 'You're the kind of a man we like, Pete. You're outa sight! What yeh goin' to buy this time, dear?'

'An't'ing yehs wants!' said the man in an abandonment of goodwill. His countenance shone with the true spirit of benevolence. He was in the proper mood of missionaries. He would have fraternized with obscure Hottentots. And above all, he was overwhelmed in tenderness for his friends, who were all illustrious.

'An't'ing yehs wants!' repeated he, waving his hands with beneficent recklessness. 'I'm good f'ler, girls, an' if an'body treats me right I— Here,' called he through an open door to a waiter, 'bring girls drinks. What 'ill yehs have, girls? An't'ing yehs want.'

The waiter glanced in with the disgusted look of the man who serves intoxicants for the man who takes too much of them. He nodded his head shortly at the order from each individual, and went.

'W're havin' great time,' said the man. 'I like you girls! Yer right sort! See?'

He spoke at length and with feeling concerning the excellences of his assembled friends.

'Don' try pull man's leg, but have a good time! Das

right! Das way teh do! Now, if I s'ought yehs tryin' work me fer drinks, wouldn' buy not'ing! But yer right sort! Yehs know how ter treat a f'ler, an' I stays by yehs 'til spen' las' cent! Das right! I'm good f'ler an' I knows when an'body treats me right!'

Between the times of the arrival and departure of the waiter, the man discoursed to the women on the tender regard he felt for all living things. He laid stress upon the purity of his motives in all dealings with men in the world, and spoke of the fervour of his friendship for those who were amiable. Tears welled slowly from his eyes. His voice quavered when he spoke to his companions.

Once when the waiter was about to depart with an empty tray, the man drew a coin from his pocket and held it forth.

'Here,' said he, quite magnificently, 'here's quar'.'

The waiter kept his hands on his tray.

'I don't want yer money,' he said.

The other put forth the coin with tearful insistence.

'Here's quar'!' cried he, 'tak't! Yer goo' f'ler an' I wan' yehs tak't!'

'Come, come, now,' said the waiter, with the sullen air of a man who is forced into giving advice. 'Put yer mon in yer pocket! Yer loaded an' yehs on'y makes a fool of yerself.'

As the latter passed out of the door the man turned pathetically to the women.

'He don' know I'm goo' f'ler,' cried he, dismally.

'Never you mind, Pete, dear,' said the woman of brilliance and audacity, laying her hand with great affection upon his arm. 'Never you mind, old boy! We'll stay by you, dear!'

'Das ri'!' cried the man, his face lighting up at the soothing tones of the woman's voice. 'Das ri'; I'm goo' f'ler, an' w'en any one trea's me ri', I trea's zem ri'! See?'

'Sure!' cried the women. 'And we're not goin' back on you, old man.'

The man turned appealing eyes to the woman. He felt that if he could be convicted of a contemptible action he would die.

'Shay, Nell, I allus trea's yehs shquare, didn' I? I allus been goo' f'ler wi' yehs, ain' I, Nell?'

'Sure you have, Pete,' assented the woman. She delivered an oration to her companions. 'Yessir, that's a fact. Pete's a square fellah, he is. He never goes back on a friend. He's the right kind an' we stay by him, don't we, girls?'

'Sure!' they exclaimed. Looking lovingly at him they raised their glasses and drank his health.

'Girlsh,' said the man, beseechingly, 'I allus trea's yehs ri', didn' I? I'm goo' f'ler, ain' I, girlsh?'

'Sure!' again they chorused.

'Well,' said he finally, 'le's have nozzer drink, zen.'

'That's right,' hailed a woman, 'that's right. Yer no bloomin' jay! Yer spends yer money like a man. Dat's right.'

The man pounded the table with his quivering fists.

'Yessir,' he cried, with deep earnestness, as if some one disputed him. 'I'm goo' f'ler, an' w'en any one trea's me ri', I allus trea's—le's have nozzer drink.'

He began to beat the wood with his glass.

'Shay!' howled he, growing suddenly impatient. As the waiter did not then come, the man swelled with wrath.

'Shay!' howled he again.

The waiter appeared at the door.

'Bringsh drinksh,' said the man.

The waiter disappeared with the orders.

'Zat f'ler fool!' cried the man. 'He insul' me! I'm ge'man! Can' stan' be insul'! I'm goin' lickim when comes!'

'No, no!' cried the women, crowding about and trying

77

to subdue him. 'He's all right! He didn't mean anything! Let it go! He's a good fellah!'

'Din' he insul' me?' asked the man earnestly.

'No,' said they. 'Of course he didn't! He's all right!'

'Sure he didn' insul' me?' demanded the man, with deep anxiety in his voice.

'No, no! We know him! He's a good fellah. He didn't mean anything.'

'Well, zen,' said the man resolutely, 'I'm go' 'pol'gize!'

When the waiter came, the man struggled to the middle of the floor.

'Girlsh shed you insul' me! I shay—lie! I 'pol'gize!'

'All right,' said the waiter.

The man sat down. He felt a sleepy but strong desire to straighten things out and have a perfect understanding with everybody.

'Nell, I allus trea's yeh shquare, din' I? Yeh likes me, don' yehs, Nell? I'm goo' f'ler?'

'Sure!' said the woman.

'Yeh knows I'm stuck on yehs, don' yehs, Nell?'

'Sure!' she repeated carelessly.

Overwhelmed by a spasm of drunken adoration, he drew two or three bills from his pocket, and with the trembling fingers of an offering priest, laid them on the table before the woman.

'Yehs knows yehs kin have all I got, 'cause I'm stuck on yehs, Nell, I—I'm stuck on yehs, Nell—buy drinksh— we're havin' great time—w'en any one trea's me ri'—I —Nell—we're havin' heluva—time.'

Presently he went to sleep with his swollen face fallen forward on his chest.

The women drank and laughed, not heeding the slumbering man in the corner. Finally he lurched forward and fell groaning to the floor.

The women screamed in disgust and drew back their skirts.

'Come ahn!' cried one, starting up angrily, 'let's get out of here.'

The woman of brilliance and audacity stayed behind, taking up the bills and stuffing them into a deep, irregularly shaped pocket. A guttural snore from the recumbent man caused her to turn and look down at him.

She laughed. 'What a fool!' she said, and went.

The smoke from the lamps settled heavily down in the little compartment, obscuring the way out. The smell of oil, stifling in its intensity, pervaded the air. The wine from an overturned glass dripped softly down upon the blotches on the man's neck.

CHAPTER 19

In a room a woman sat at a table eating like a fat monk in a picture.

A soiled, unshaven man pushed open the door and entered.

'Well,' said he, 'Mag's dead.'

'What?' said the woman, her mouth filled with bread.

'Mag's dead,' repeated the man.

'Deh blazes she is!' said the woman. She continued her meal. When she finished her coffee she began to weep.

'I kin remember when her two feet was no bigger dan yer tumb, and she weared worsted boots,' moaned she.

'Well, whata dat?' said the man.

'I kin remember when she weared worsted boots,' she cried.

The neighbours began to gather in the hall, staring in at the weeping woman as if watching the contortions of a dying dog. A dozen women entered and lamented with her. Under their busy hands the room took on that appealing appearance of neatness and order with which death is greeted.

Suddenly the door opened and a woman in a black gown rushed in with outstretched arms. 'Ah, poor Mary!' she cried, and tenderly embraced the moaning one.

'Ah, what ter'ble affliction is dis!' continued she. Her vocabulary was derived from mission churches. 'Me poor Mary, how I feel fer yehs! Ah, what a ter'ble affliction is a disobed'ent chile.'

Her good, motherly face was wet with tears. She trembled in eagerness to express her sympathy. The mourner sat with bowed head, rocking her body to and fro, and crying out in a high, strained voice that sounded like a dirge on some forlorn pipe.

'I kin remember when she weared worsted boots an' her two feets was no bigger dan yer tumb an' she weared worsted boots, Miss Smith,' she cried, raising her streaming eyes.

'Ah, me poor Mary!' sobbed the woman in black. With low, coddling cries, she sank on her knees by the mourner's chair, and put her arms about her. The other women began to groan in different keys.

'Yer poor misguided chil' is gone now, Mary, an' let us hope it's fer deh bes'. Yeh'll fergive her now, Mary, won't yehs, dear, all her disobed'ence? All her t'ankless behaviour to her mudder an' all her badness? She's gone where her ter'ble sins will be judged.'

The woman in black raised her face and paused. The inevitable sunlight came streaming in at the window and shed a ghastly cheerfulness upon the faded hues of the room. Two or three of the spectators were sniffing, and one was weeping loudly. The mourner arose and staggered into the other room. In a moment she emerged with a pair of faded baby shoes held in the hollow of her hand.

'I kin remember when she used to wear dem!' cried she. The women burst anew into cries as if they had all been stabbed. The mourner turned to the soiled and unshaven man.

'Jimmie, boy, go git yer sister! Go git yer sister an' we'll put deh boots on her feets!'

'Dey won't fit her now, yeh fool,' said the man.

'Go git yer sister, Jimmie!' shrieked the woman, confronting him fiercely.

The man swore sullenly. He went over to a corner and slowly began to put on his coat. He took his hat and went out, with a dragging, reluctant step.

The woman in black came forward and again besought the mourner.

'Yeh'll fergive her, Mary! Yeh'll fergive yer bad, bad chil'! Her life was a curse an' her days were black, an' yeh'll fergive yer bad girl? She's gone where her sins will be judged.'

'She's gone where her sins will be judged!' cried the other women, like a choir at a funeral.

'Deh Lord gives and deh Lord takes away,' said the woman in black, raising her eyes to the sunbeams.

'Deh Lord gives and deh Lord takes away,' responded the others.

'Yeh'll fergive her, Mary?' pleaded the woman in black. The mourner essayed to speak but her voice gave way. She shook her great shoulders frantically, in an agony of grief. The tears seemed to scald her face. Finally her voice came and arose in a scream of pain.

'Oh, yes, I'll fergive her! I'll fergive her!'